BOOK THREE

☆

S.O.S.

LOOK FOR MORE ADVENTURE FROM
GORDON KORMAN

TITANIC
BOOK ONE: UNSINKABLE
BOOK TWO: COLLISION COURSE
BOOK THREE: S.O.S.

KIDNAPPED
BOOK ONE: THE ABDUCTION
BOOK TWO: THE SEARCH
BOOK THREE: THE RESCUE

ON THE RUN
BOOK ONE: CHASING THE FALCONERS
BOOK TWO: THE FUGITIVE FACTOR
BOOK THREE: NOW YOU SEE THEM, NOW YOU DON'T
BOOK FOUR: THE STOWAWAY SOLUTION
BOOK FIVE: PUBLIC ENEMIES
BOOK SIX: HUNTING THE HUNTER

DIVE
BOOK ONE: THE DISCOVERY
BOOK TWO: THE DEEP
BOOK THREE: THE DANGER

EVEREST
BOOK ONE: THE CONTEST
BOOK TWO: THE CLIMB
BOOK THREE: THE SUMMIT

ISLAND
BOOK ONE: SHIPWRECK
BOOK TWO: SURVIVAL
BOOK THREE: ESCAPE

TITANIC

BOOK THREE

S.O.S.

GORDON KORMAN

SCHOLASTIC INC.

NEW YORK   TORONTO   LONDON   AUCKLAND

SYDNEY   MEXICO CITY   NEW DELHI   HONG KONG

ISBN 978-0-545-12333-4

12 11 10 9 8 7   13 14 15 16/0

Printed in the U.S.A.   40
First printing, September 2011

The text type was set in Sabon.
Book design by Tim Hall

FOR LEO

PROLOGUE

RMS *CALIFORNIAN* —
MONDAY, APRIL 15, 1912, 12:15 A.M.

The small ocean liner sat at rest on the still, glassy waters of the North Atlantic.

It was not the flat calm that had brought the *Californian* to a dead stop, but rather the mass quantities of field ice that lay about. Captain Lord was unwilling to proceed until daylight illuminated the hazards that surrounded his vessel.

The ship had been transmitting ice warnings all day. It was little wonder that Marconi operator Evans had decided to go to bed early.

While Evans slept, his station was manned by Third Officer Groves. By 12:15 A.M., the silence from the headphones grew tiresome, and Groves, too, gave up for the night.

If his tea had been a little hotter, and he'd had to drink it a little more slowly, he might have had time to remember that the *Californian*'s wireless set had to be wound manually.

A few turns of the crank, and Third Officer Groves would have heard the message: *CQD MGY.*

CQD meant "come quickly — distress." *MGY* represented the call letters of the RMS *Titanic*, the largest, grandest, and most celebrated ocean liner in the world.

The *Titanic* was also stopped in the water, less than ten miles away.

And she was sinking.

CHAPTER ONE

RMS *TITANIC* —
MONDAY, APRIL 15, 1912, 12:15 A.M.

Captain E. J. Smith noticed it the instant he stepped onto the boat deck. The bow was down. It would be imperceptible to all but the most experienced seaman. Yet to the commodore of the White Star Line, it was all too glaring and all too real. Also real was the tilt in the deck. Smith's sea legs had never failed him before — just as he'd never before sent a distress call . . . until tonight.

He took only a few seconds to appreciate once more the most magnificent ship that had ever sailed the seas. The largest, the most technologically advanced, the most luxurious, and — his lip quivered ever so slightly — the safest.

This was to have been his final voyage. Now he was certain of that fact.

But he had no time for reflection. There were

decisions to be made. It was the captain's job to make them.

He walked back to the bridge and faced Thomas Andrews, the *Titanic*'s designer.

"Mr. Andrews, how many lifeboats do we have?" he asked.

The shipbuilder's expression was impassive. "Twenty, sir, including four Engelhardt collapsibles. Capacity one thousand one hundred and seventy-eight."

The captain nodded grimly. The passengers and crew numbered 2,223.

Junior Steward Alfie Huggins was soaked to the skin with icy seawater, but sweat poured from him as never before. With passengers Sophie Bronson and Juliana Glamm in tow, he raced aft in an attempt to escape the sinking bow of the mighty liner. They pounded along D Deck until a solid bulkhead barred their progress. A companion stair led them up to C, and they sprinted across the open well deck, dodging scattered ice fragments, some as large as steamer trunks.

Sophie's slippered foot came down on a chunk, and she nearly took a spill. Alfie hauled her upright without losing a step. The shard skittered away, colliding with many others.

"It's hard to believe *this* is what damaged a ship this size!" Sophie gasped.

The ice had broken off a huge berg — now behind them — that had torn a three-hundred-foot gash in the *Titanic*'s belly.

"Damaged, yes, but the ship is unsinkable," Juliana panted. "Isn't it?"

The image that appeared in Alfie's mind was his father in Number 5 Boiler Room, waist-deep in water. His exact words: *We're going to find out.*

They entered the ship's towering superstructure, dashing down a first-class companionway. Stewards filled the corridor, knocking on doors, helping bewildered passengers into bulky life belts. The general air was complaint and irritation.

"I say, it's the middle of the night!"

"What is the purpose of this disturbance?"

"Why should we don life belts? God himself could not sink this ship!"

"It's just a precaution," Alfie heard a fellow steward soothe. "The captain has ordered everyone up on the boat deck. And dress warmly, please. The night is very cold."

"All the more reason to remain in my cabin," declared an elderly lady.

The *Titanic*'s first class was filled with the rich and

pampered of the world. They were not accustomed to being discommoded and marched about by mere servants.

The stewards were patient and unfailingly polite. But they did not take no for an answer.

Alfie and the girls dashed out of the companion-way and wheeled around to ascend the majestic grand staircase. There they found Second Officer Charles Herbert Lightoller heading briskly down the richly carpeted steps.

"Huggins," Lightoller said, "why are you not attending to your passengers?"

"Miss Sophie and Miss Juliana *are* my passengers," Alfie tried to explain.

But by this time, Lightoller had gotten a good look at the three of them. "Why are you all wet?"

"The bow is making water, sir!" Alfie explained breathlessly. "They're on the pumps in Number 5 Boiler Room, but Number 6 is completely swamped!"

"And you took these young ladies with you," Lightoller commented wryly. "How gallant. Get them to the boat deck — with life belts, if you please. Then see to the rest of your passengers."

"Mr. Lightoller — is it really so serious?" Juliana asked timidly.

The officer's expression was grave. "Take a look at

the state of your pretty gown, and you'll have your answer. Now move along."

Alfie started up the stairs. "Follow me!"

"I'm not going to the boat deck," Sophie told him. "At least, not yet. I have to find Mother."

"And I my father," Juliana agreed. Her eyes narrowed. "And I have a pretty good idea where he might be."

☆

In the first-class lounge, there was no mention of icebergs or life belts — in fact, no sense of urgency at all. Men talked and played cards. Waiters served drinks. A cloud of cigar and pipe smoke hung in the air of the mahogany-paneled room. If the occupants had any idea of the commotion that roiled the other parts of the ship, they gave no indication.

Juliana found her father in the exact spot where he'd spent nine-tenths of the voyage thus far: at the large table in the center of the lounge, deeply embroiled in a high-stakes poker game.

She addressed him quietly. "Papa, we must go to the boat deck at once."

Rodney, Earl of Glamford, did not even look up at her as he examined his cards. "Why ever should I want to do that?" he murmured, lost in concentration.

"The captain has ordered it," Juliana persisted. "All passengers are to don life belts —"

"Life belts?" She had her father's attention now. He stared at her a moment and then chuckled. "My dear Julie, someone is having you on. What earthly purpose could life belts serve aboard the *Titanic*?"

"We've struck an iceberg —"

"Everyone knows that. We felt the jar. Simsbury spilled his drink on the table and we had to send for a new deck of cards."

"Papa, the ship is filling up with water!"

"Nonsense. The *Titanic* is unsinkable. Besides" — he dropped his voice to a whisper — "I'm *winning*. I believe my luck is finally beginning to change."

CHAPTER TWO

"No." Mrs. Willingham was adamant. "I will not leave without my Muffin."

Muffin turned out to be a nervous, nasty Pomeranian, who could not be pried loose from the fabric of Alfie's trousers.

"It is the captain's orders," Alfie insisted, trying to shake the dog from his leg. "All passengers to the boat deck."

She was unmoved. "Muffin is a passenger."

Alfie gave in. "Very well, madam, but keep her in the pocket of your cloak. We have no life belts for pets. And please detach him from my cuff. I have more staterooms to visit."

Muffin was lured off of him with a bonbon, and Alfie hurried along the A-Deck passageway.

A woman grabbed him in front of A-22. "What's happening? Are we abandoning ship?"

Alfie gulped. "Oh, I expect not. It's just a precaution."

"In that case, I'll not wake my children," she decided. "They are ever so cranky when their sleep is interrupted."

Alfie was torn. The stewards had been warned not to spread panic. Yet how could he abide leaving children asleep when he knew the bow was filling with water?

"By all means, awaken them," he said finally. "This is going to be a jolly good adventure. You wouldn't want them to miss it."

Having done his best, he hurried along to the next cabin.

"Alfie, thank the Lord you're here!" Another steward, Jules Tryhorn, stood in a first-class stateroom, engaged in a monumental struggle to place a life belt around Major Mountjoy. The major was so portly that the device simply would not fasten in the back.

"Bless my soul!" the major exclaimed, his mutton-chop whiskers wagging above his jowls. "I do seem to have rounded out a bit, due to the magnificent table set aboard this fine ship. What's to be done?"

Alfie surveyed the situation. "If you pull from the back," he told Tryhorn, "and I push from the front . . ."

"Oh, I *say*!" The major's voice suddenly jumped an octave as the two stewards heaved with all their might to encase his girth within the life belt's circumference. There was a click, and he was in it, for better or worse.

"Well done, lads!" Mountjoy exclaimed, panting a little more than usual. He started out of the stateroom in a penguinlike waddle. "Next time, I promise I shall be as fit as a fiddle and not cause you so much difficulty."

Alfie shuddered. Next time!

He continued down the passageway and found himself facing the brass plate that read A-17. Just the sight of it made his blood run cold.

Less than an hour ago, Mr. Masterson of A-17 had tried to kill him — and Miss Sophie, too. Incredibly, this was far from the worst thing Mr. Masterson had ever done. During the voyage, Alfie had uncovered evidence proving without a doubt that the man was the ghastly murderer known as Jack the Ripper. The Whitechapel killer of 1888 was traveling aboard the *Titanic* to see a New York doctor who could repair his crippled legs.

I'll not knock on that door, Alfie told himself. *I'll do nothing to save this terrible beast so he can live to terrorize and kill again.*

It was the first time he admitted, even to himself, that there might be some saving to be done on the *Titanic* this night. The captain hadn't ordered passengers to the boat deck in order for them to take in the sea air.

But as he passed, the door to A-17 opened a crack and a wary eye peered out.

"What's the commotion, boy?"

"Nothing to concern yourself about," Alfie replied evenly. "Pleasant dreams."

Tryhorn came up behind Alfie. "Are you daft, man? The captain has ordered everyone into their life belts! We're all to assemble on the boat deck!"

Masterson scowled. "What — because of the iceberg?"

"We're damaged," Tryhorn explained. "Although no one knows how badly."

Masterson reached for his crutch. "I require assistance with my life belt."

"You'll not have it from me," Alfie replied stiffly, moving on to the next door.

Tryhorn followed after him. "What's the matter with you, Alfie? I admit he's an unpleasant person, but you can't abandon a poor cripple in an emergency!"

This was no time to go into detail about the scrapbook that proved this monster's identity. "Save your sympathy for someone who deserves it!" Alfie snapped, and then knocked on the door of stateroom A-16.

☆

The first thing Paddy Burns saw as he reached the boat deck was a lifeboat swinging out on its davit into position for loading.

It's really happening, thought the young Irish stowaway. *I was right, I was.*

The unsinkable *Titanic* was sinking, just like his poor friend Daniel had said it could, back in Belfast, a lifetime ago. And now some of the richest toffs in the world were huddled here as the sailors worked the boats into position.

Paddy's practiced eyes scanned the crowd. What a feast for a pickpocket like himself! Every millionaire on two continents, crammed together in one place, nervous and distracted. A fellow could retire on the pickings laid out before him now — if only the boat wasn't sinking, which it was. And they all — from John Jacob Astor with one hundred and fifty million American dollars, to Paddy without a penny to bless himself — would soon have problems more pressing than a lifted brooch or purse.

"Paddy — over here!"

Paddy pushed through the milling throng to join

Sophie and her mother, Amelia Bronson, the famous suffragist.

"Thank goodness you made it out!" Sophie cried. "I thought we'd never see you again! How is it on E Deck?"

"There is no E Deck," Paddy replied grimly. "At least, not in the bow. The water's up to the ceiling."

Mrs. Bronson watched Boat 6 come even with the rail. "You stay with us, Paddy. I'll make sure you're not denied your rightful place on a lifeboat just because you're a stowaway."

Paddy looked around, uneasy. "I've hidden in one of those boats, and I've counted them, too. Unless they've got a magician pulling them out of a silk hat, they won't have enough space for everybody."

"Surely not!" exclaimed Sophie, shocked. "The White Star Line would never play dice with the lives of its passengers! Look around you. Do these seem like the kinds of people who could be denied a seat on a lifeboat?"

Paddy *did* look around. She was absolutely right. The names were famous the world over — Astor, Guggenheim, Rothes, Straus. Business tycoons and titled nobility. These people expected top treatment.

All at once, it dawned on Paddy: The swells of first class were not the only passengers aboard the *Titanic*.

There were more than seven hundred third-class passengers — Irish, Scandinavians, Italians, and emigrants from dozens of other places, hoping for a better future in America. These were good, hardworking people, the salt of the earth. They had every bit as much right to life as Colonel John Jacob Astor.

But not one of them was on the top deck, awaiting a place on the *Titanic*'s lifeboats.

CHAPTER THREE

RMS *CARPATHIA* —
MONDAY, APRIL 15, 1912, 12:25 A.M.

It was him again.

Marconi operator Harold Cottam looked up at the doorway of the wireless shack and there he was — young, eager, hard to get rid of, even after midnight. *Especially* after midnight, when things were quiet, and Cottam couldn't really complain that he was too busy.

Drazen Curcovic, age fourteen, the son of a Croatian diplomat, stepped into the small office, gazing worshipfully up at Cottam. "I thought perhaps this might be a convenient moment. . . ."

"A bit late, isn't it?" Cottam said hopefully.

Drazen looked so disappointed that the wireless operator had to relent. On the first day of the *Carpathia*'s voyage, the boy had turned up at the Marconi room and declared, "Of all the sailors on this ship, it is *you* I admire most!" And he must have meant it, because his adulation since that day had become downright embarrassing. Drazen was so enthralled with the new technology that he worshipped anyone associated with it. Never mind that the salary of a Marconi operator was less than five pounds per voyage. The diplomat's son was determined to learn every detail of wireless communication.

Cottam sighed. "Very well, lad. You can take over the set for a few minutes. But you're not likely to hear much in the wee hours of a Monday morning."

Overjoyed, Drazen donned the headset and took Cottam's place at the desk. The expression on his face was pure bliss despite the fact that all he could hear was white noise and the occasional crackle of static.

Cottam put on water for tea and began to glance through a days-old New York newspaper. A gasp from Drazen recaptured his attention. The boy was standing, white as a sheet.

"I — I think you should hear this, Mr. Cottam!"

"Now, now," Cottam lectured. "When you wear that headset, you and only you are responsible for the messages that come in on your watch."

"In that case," Drazen replied, "wake the captain."

"You're barmy!" Cottam exclaimed with a short laugh. "Why ever would I do that?"

"It's a C-Q-D!" Drazen said tensely, struggling to translate the Morse code Cottam had taught him. "*Struck an iceberg and sinking by the head* . . . the call letters are M-G-Y!"

"M-G-Y?" repeated Cottam. "Why, that's —" He rushed over to a small ledger and began leafing through the pages. "Good God, it's the *Titanic*!"

☆

Water trickled down the metal work stairs as Paddy pounded from D Deck to E. About halfway along, his hobnail boots slipped out from under him on the slick steps and he made a short, painful descent, bouncing on his bottom. He landed with a splash into frigid water, but jumped right up and began to slosh his way aft along the broad passageway known as Scotland Road.

It seemed a very long way before his feet came down on dry deck. He was puffing, too, as if slogging uphill — which, in a way, he was. As the *Titanic*'s nose dipped lower, the simple act of moving aft became a climb.

Scotland Road, normally a busy place, was deserted. At this point in the crisis, all crew members were at their stations. The picture was very different, however, at the base of the third-class staircase. That was a mob scene. All of steerage had been assembled, and an agitated clamor in a dozen different languages echoed off the unadorned bulkheads.

The stewards were putting people into life belts, but many of the emigrants who didn't understand English were resisting help. The physical struggle of it rippled through the tight crowd like a shoving match.

"Mrs. Rankin!" Paddy began to work his way through the chaotic assemblage, searching for the family that had helped hide him from the White Star Line.

A hand reached out from the throng and spun him around as he passed. A moment later, he was in Mrs. Rankin's arms.

"Paddy, I took an extra life belt! I knew you'd come back!"

"What's going on down here?" Paddy asked her. "Why aren't they moving you up to the boat deck with the other passengers?"

"They took a small group of women up a few minutes ago, but that's all," she replied. "Why, Paddy? What do you know? What's going on?"

Paddy was distraught. "They're swinging out life-boats, they are! I'll bet the loading has already started! How can they leave people down here?"

"Why do you bother yourself to ask that question?" she cried in despair. "We're foreigners. The English don't care a whit about us!"

"That they don't!" exploded Curran — at seventeen, the eldest of the four Rankin boys. "Why are we being held here? Why can't we go to the boat deck?"

"It's for your own safety," called Mr. Steptoe, senior-most of the third-class stewards.

"How does it save us to be belowdecks on a sinking ship?" someone shouted.

"Oh, so you know better than the captain himself?" Steptoe snapped. "For one thing, getting to the boat deck isn't as simple as you make it out to be. Do you think these stairs lead straight up to first class? Well, they don't! If I turn you lot loose, you'll get lost. And then where will you be?"

Paddy spoke up. "I know how to get to the boat deck."

Steptoe stared at him in sudden recognition. "You're the stowaway!"

"What are you going to do, then?" Paddy scoffed.

"Put me in the brig? It's underwater, don't you know!" He turned to the crowd. "Which is where you'll all be if you don't get out of here! Now, who's with me?"

A nervous indecision rippled through the crowd. Why should anyone take the word of a single bedraggled Irish boy, soaked to the skin?

Mrs. Rankin broke the silence. "Me and mine are going with you, Paddy!" She faced the throng. "I'll not be telling you what to do. But you might want to think about how the English have been treating us since the dawn of history."

The Rankin boys followed their mother and Paddy to the third-class staircase. A few others joined them timidly, wilting under the stewards' disapproval.

Steptoe hurried over to bar their way. "I'll not allow it."

The two elder Rankin boys lifted him, each at an elbow, and set him down again amid the throng. Several other stewards started forward, but the hostile crowd moved to cut them off from the steps.

"There's a natural order to how these things are done!" Steptoe raged. "Why are you supporting these line-jumpers? It's *your* places they're taking, and creating chaos at a time when we need discipline! When it is our turn, we will be called!"

Paddy paused at the first landing, shepherding his group up the stairs. Perhaps thirty people, including the Rankins, were with him. The others, hundreds of them, milled about on E Deck, looking worried, uneasy. In spite of the many lessons their hard lives had surely taught them, they were choosing to be sheep — to obey the instructions of men in fancy uniforms over what their common sense must have been telling them.

"Which way, Paddy?" called Aidan Rankin from above.

Paddy raced to take the lead, and the group surged up the staircase, spilling out onto the aft well deck. All eyes were immediately drawn to the boat deck, three levels above. There swung the lifeboats, ringing the superstructure like the beads of a rosary. Even from that distance they could make out the first-class ladies, wrapped in heavy cloaks against the bitter cold, being loaded aboard.

"Are we truly sinking?" shrilled a young woman hugging her baby.

"Believe it," Paddy said grimly. "Do you think the

crew would inconvenience those rich swells for anything less?"

Mrs. Rankin looked around in alarm. "Isn't that just like the English? They build their death trap, and *we're* the ones who have to suffer for it."

Curran nodded fervently. "Ma's right. Those lifeboats might as well be in God's own heaven for all we can get to them from here."

"Follow me!" ordered Paddy.

He guided the group out of the well deck via a steep companion stair. There, behind a tall, horn-shaped ventilator, a crew ladder led straight up the *Titanic*'s superstructure.

One by one, they made the climb. The woman handed her baby to Aidan as Paddy and Curran helped her over the rail. They were on A Deck now, just one level below the dangling lifeboats.

The sounds of chaos on the boat deck were audible now — the anxious babble of passengers punctuated by urgent shouted instructions from the crew.

"I'll not allow you to put me on that thing so I can catch my death of cold!" declared one woman's authoritative voice above them. A chorus of agreement rang out.

"Will you listen to that?" said Mrs. Rankin in a

subdued tone. "Not all of us bleat like sheep, taking orders from anyone in a monkey suit."

Paddy nodded wisely. "Those first-class toffs stand up for themselves, they do. Even if it's for the privilege of drowning."

CHAPTER FOUR

Paddy tried the French door leading to the Verandah Café.

Locked.

He kicked out of one of his hobnail boots and, wielding it like a hammer, used the heel to smash one pane. Then he reached inside and flipped the lock. The door swung wide, and the group from steerage streamed inside. All urgency was momentarily forgotten as they took in the genteel elegance and luxury of the café, with its ivy-covered walls and immaculate crystal, silver, and china.

The young mother crossed herself. "Heaven itself must look like this."

"Heaven isn't sinking," Paddy reminded her. "Keep moving."

A tuxedo-clad waiter stepped out of the shadows. "You can't be here! This is first class!" His eyes took in the punched-out pane and the glass shards on the floor. "That's company property!"

Curran stared at him. "Are you daft, man? There's a lot more broken than your fancy door!"

"You'll have to pay for that!" the waiter insisted.

Paddy laughed without humor. "Tell the White Star Line to send me the reckoning."

The group trailed through the Verandah into the deep oak paneling of the smoking room. To their amazement, there were several elderly gentlemen, life belts over their evening clothes, puffing peacefully on pipes and cigars.

"Don't they know?" Mrs. Rankin whispered.

Paddy shrugged. "The rich are different."

They passed from one sumptuous room to another, silent in their awe. Paddy had become used to the splendor of first class, but the rest had never seen its like. It was a far cry from their spartan accommodations aboard the ship and the homes they had left behind — tiny cabins with dirt floors and smoky peat fires.

They finally emerged beneath the third smokestack and found themselves absorbed into a scene of pure bedlam. Humanity teemed all around them — the world's rich and famous, in a bizarre assortment of clothing. Some still wore elegant evening attire.

Others were in nightdress, complete with silk bath-robes and bedroom slippers. Most were wrapped in furs, cloaks, coats, and even the blankets from their beds. If there was panic, it did not show. The general air was one of annoyance at the inconvenience of being roused from their sleep or dragged from their evening activities to stand in close quarters in the icy cold of the night. Snatches of conversation rose above the din.

"If this is a lifeboat drill, I think it is singularly ill-timed."

"No, that's not it. Some fool steered into an iceberg, and we've thrown a propeller blade."

"I expected better from Captain Smith."

"Why should I even dream of getting into an open boat when I can stay in my suite where it's warm and comfortable?"

"This never would have happened on the *Mauritania*."

"I shall write a strong letter of protest to the White Star Line."

Most bewildering of all was the presence of the orchestra from the first-class dining saloon. The musicians were assembled in the midst of the crowd, playing lively ragtime as if nothing were amiss.

"What's the matter with these people?" demanded

Mrs. Rankin. "Don't they understand that we're sinking?"

"They probably don't believe it," Paddy replied, raising his voice to be heard over the music. "How can anything bad happen to you when you've got piles of money?"

They pushed through the throng to where Chief Officer Wilde was trying to help an elderly lady over the rail into a precariously balanced lifeboat.

"I cannot do it, and I don't see why I should!" she shrilled.

"Madam, you must," said Wilde. "It is the captain's orders."

With a cry, she tumbled over the rail and into the wooden craft.

"Are there any more women and children?" the chief officer called.

Paddy pushed Mrs. Rankin forward, and Wilde helped her into the boat. Her sons Sean and Finnbar were lifted in after her, but the chief officer stepped in front of Aidan and Curran. "Women and children first," he directed.

"They *are* children — *my* children!" Mrs. Rankin cried.

"They may try for a later boat," Wilde insisted. "Right now, the order is women and children."

Mrs. Rankin's eyes widened in horror. It was a terrible dilemma. If she tried to keep her family together, and took herself and her younger sons off the boat, she might be dooming all of them.

"It's okay, Ma," Curran called. "Don't worry about us. There'll be another boat."

"There you go, ma'am," Wilde reassured her. "Your boys have the right of it. You'll see them later." He waved to a fellow seaman who was approaching. "Take over."

Paddy watched as the crowd parted and the new man arrived. It was Second Officer Lightoller — and that was bad news. Lightoller would recognize Paddy as the stowaway he'd been chasing for days.

Paddy melted into the throng and worked his way forward, marveling at the absence of any sense of urgency. Were rich people really such fools? They were more put out by the bulky and unsightly life belts than the fact that the ship was sinking!

"The order is women and children only!" came the odd Welsh accent of Fifth Officer Lowe in a warning tone.

Paddy turned back to see Kevin Gilhooley and his bodyguard, Seamus, attempting to board the fifth officer's boat.

Not twenty minutes before, Paddy had released

these gangsters from a cell as the brig filled with water. He was still berating himself for doing so. He believed that the Gilhooley organization had murdered Daniel, his best and only friend back in Belfast. And aboard the *Titanic*, they had made a deliberate — and very nearly successful — attempt to kill Paddy.

But to drown like rats in a cage . . .

Paddy had been unable to bring himself to let it happen — even to thugs like those two.

Seamus held up a fistful of banknotes, but Lowe waved it away, insulted and outraged. "Stand away and wait like gentlemen!"

"If you won't accept an honest gratuity," Gilhooley shouted, "perhaps the favor of not throwing you over the side will make an impression!"

"You'll not board this boat unless God or Captain Smith himself orders it!" The fifth officer reached into his uniform pocket and produced a small pistol.

Seamus and Gilhooley backed off, and Paddy stepped around a corner to avoid being seen. He had saved the two gangsters, but he still feared them.

He found himself peering in one of the large gymnasium windows. To his surprise, the room was occupied — and by very distinguished company. Colonel John Jacob Astor, the wealthiest man aboard, sat with his young wife on a small exercise bench.

With a gold-handled pocketknife, he had cut open a life belt and was showing his bride the cork inside — without a thought to the fact that some poor soul might need the now-ruined belt. Indeed, the rich were different.

Paddy's thoughts immediately returned to the third-class general room — the hundreds of steerage passengers huddled like sheep. They had chosen to stay below and wait for "their turn."

With the likes of the Astors aboard, would their turn ever come?

CHAPTER FIVE

RMS *TITANIC* —
MONDAY, APRIL 15, 1912, 12:35 A.M.

Mr. Masterson thumped along Scotland Road, moving as fast as his crutch would carry him. Despite his ruined legs, he felt strangely invigorated and alive. This night, for the first time in twenty-four years, he had acted as his alter ego, Jack the Ripper. Alas, he had not been successful, but that was only due to his infirmity. This would all change when he reached New York. After his doctor's miracle surgery, he would be whole again, and ready to resume his life's work.

But that horrible Bronson girl and Huggins, the steward, had both seen his scrapbook. He could not allow it to fall into the hands of someone who might present it to the authorities. After the collision with the iceberg, there was a good chance they might have to abandon ship. In that case, any salvage operation might come across his precious souvenirs, prompted by the accusations of those dreadful young people. If his true identity were proven in a court of law, he would undoubtedly dance at the end of a rope.

That was the reason for this mad dash to E Deck. He must get down to the baggage hold to recover his scrapbook. His vital mission must not end before it could be reborn.

He had barely passed the first access ladder that led down to the boiler rooms when his crutch suddenly slipped out from under his arm, and he went down with a startled cry. He hit the deck, not with the painful wallop he expected, but with an icy splash.

What? Water?

He pulled himself back to his unsteady stance and stared ahead. Good Lord, why hadn't he noticed it before? E Deck was on a slant, the way a sandy beach gave way to lapping sea.

And if this was happening *here* — this far aft, then . . .

Masterson was no sailor, but the image that formed in his mind could not have been clearer. The *Titanic*'s bow was dipping below the ocean's surface, filling with water. This supposedly unsinkable vessel was *sinking*!

There was no longer any reason to worry about the

scrapbook. The hold was surely swamped, and his incriminating memoir was destroyed. He felt a momentary sense of loss that was replaced in short order by a second conclusion: The *Titanic* was headed for the bottom of the ocean. His most urgent task was to get himself aboard one of the lifeboats.

Nothing must interfere with his destiny. Not even the death of the greatest ship the world ever knew.

☆

"*Lower away!*"

The first starboard-side boat was on her way down, descending in jerky fits and starts as the sailors allowed the heavy line to pay out. No one had considered the possibility that the lifeboats might actually be used; therefore the crew had not invested any time training how to use them. Modern shipbuilding had gone far beyond that.

Or so we believed, Alfie reflected ruefully.

He peered over the side and was astounded to find the dangling craft more than half empty. He turned to one of the crewmen at the ropes. "Why didn't you fill her?"

"Oh, so you know more about it than Mr. Lightoller!" the sailor shot back, his arms working like pistons.

"Then why didn't *he* fill her?" Alfie cried. "There's not thirty souls aboard!"

"Twenty-eight, Huggins, to be precise." The second officer squared his shoulders to Alfie. "In a boat with a capacity of sixty-five. Not that I'm obligated to explain my orders to the likes of you."

"But *why*? There are so many that need to be rescued!"

"Too much weight could buckle a wooden hull," Lightoller explained with his customary confident decisiveness. "I've sent the bosun's mate and a few hands down to the lower gangway door. We can fill the boats from there."

"What if they never find the lower gangway door?" Alfie demanded.

"Don't be absurd, man. Why shouldn't they?"

"The forward compartments are filling up and spilling over!" Alfie told him in agitation. "The lower decks are awash! It's getting worse every minute!"

The second officer digested this thoughtfully. "If that's true, Huggins, then it would appear that we are all in rather a tight corner."

"A tight corner!" Alfie echoed. "You might have sent your men to find a door that's underwater! Won't you at least call them back? I'll go myself, if it pleases you!"

"Your responsibility is to your passengers, Huggins."

"My passengers are awaiting their turns on the boats, Mr. Lightoller. There's nothing more I can do for them now."

"Your duty is to see to their comfort," Lightoller reminded him.

"See to their comfort?" The young steward had spent most of the voyage scared to death of the *Titanic*'s no-nonsense, by-the-book second officer. But this lecture on responsibility and duty was nothing short of ridiculous. "They are shivering in life belts and pajamas, as their dream ship sinks into the waves! I can't imagine a single one of them being very comfortable, Mr. Lightoller! You'll have to put me on report!"

"You are insubordinate, Huggins," Lightoller told him, his voice under tight control.

"Yes, sir, I suppose I am." He wheeled on the second officer and started below. The stairs were noticeably tilted — each step not quite where he expected it to be. Forward along Scotland Road he hurried, keeping an eye out for the bosun's mate and his group. But Alfie had always known his real reason for coming down here — Fireman John Huggins, Alfie's father.

The *Titanic*'s hull was divided into sixteen sealed compartments. It was the feature that supposedly rendered the great ship unsinkable. But what was happening in reality was that each compartment was filling up, and then spilling over the top into the next. The result was that water seemed to be coming from all directions, even trickling down from above.

Alfie swung a leg into the opening and descended the crew ladder to the boiler rooms, trying to ignore the relentless icy dribble from above. The scene on the orlop deck, however, soon erased all thoughts of his own discomfort. The combination of white-hot fire and waist-deep water had conjured a cloud of steam as dense as porridge.

He took off his sodden jacket and waved it wildly in an attempt to disperse the scorching fog. As his vision cleared, he took in the *Titanic*'s black gang, the water near to their chests, still stoking the ship's insatiable furnaces. They all looked alike, drenched and soot-stained, yet Alfie would have known his own da among a hundred such men. John Huggins had traded his shovel for a pump handle, and was striving to beat back the ever-encroaching sea.

"What are you doing, Da? You can't pump away the whole ocean!"

His father paused in his efforts, and turned on his

son in a fury. "Get out of here, you bloody fool! I didn't give you life so you could throw it away!"

Shocked, Alfie stared at him. "Get out yourself! You're not doing any good down here! Nobody needs your engines! The ship's stopped dead! She's not going anywhere but down!"

"That's where you're wrong, boy. These fires don't just run engines. They're keeping the lights on. And power to the wireless equipment so we can send distress calls. We're firemen, and this is what we do."

"But how will you escape?" Alfie cried. "You're nine decks below the nearest boat!"

His father's face was the picture of weariness and resignation. "I'll not be getting out."

"*No!*" Alfie screamed. "There may be things worth dying for, but the White Star Line isn't one of them!"

In this of all places, there was a peculiar dignity in the way John Huggins carried himself. "At a time like this, a man realizes what his life is really about. Being away at sea, I wasn't much of a husband or a father. What I had — *all* I had — was my job. And that's what I'll be doing when I take my last breath on this ship."

Alfie didn't want to cry, but once the tears started, he couldn't hold them back. "You're more than a job to *me*!"

A convulsive sob rattled the soot-blackened stoker. It was the first time Alfie had ever seen so much emotion coming from his father. "And you to me, boy! That's why you have to promise me you'll survive this night. Now go. And I'll keep the lights burning long enough for you to find a lifeboat. As long as you see the lights, you'll know that's me."

They shared a brief embrace. There was no time for more. Then the father was back on the pump, and the son who had made the promise was splashing toward the access ladder, his eyes blinded by much more than steam.

CHAPTER SIX

RMS *TITANIC* —
MONDAY, APRIL 15, 1912, 12:40 A.M.

The voices on the boat deck were becoming a little less quiet and civilized as the tilt of the ship grew obvious to even the unseasoned. But Captain Smith heard none of this. He peered through binoculars at a set of lights on the horizon — lights that could only belong to a steamer.

"Why doesn't she answer?" he mused aloud. "She can't be more than eight, perhaps ten miles away." He turned to the sailor at his side who was signaling with a Morse lamp. "Are you getting any response?"

"Negative, sir. But she doesn't seem to be moving off."

Smith grimaced. "She doesn't seem to be moving at all. Surely she sees us."

Assistant Wireless Officer Harold Bride appeared

on the bridge, a bulky life belt fastened over his uniform. "Good news, Captain. The *Carpathia* has responded, and she's coming hard. She'll be here by daybreak."

"Young man," said the commodore of the White Star Line, "*we* shall not be here by daybreak. Haven't you heard from anyone closer?" He pointed at the distant lights. "Her, for instance?"

The young operator squinted into the night. "Not a peep, sir."

"Are you certain?"

Bride nodded. "At this distance, her signal would have blown my ears off."

"Very well." The captain nodded shortly. "Continue to transmit our C-Q-D."

"Aye, sir," said Bride. "And I might even give the new call a try — S-O-S." He smiled with grim amusement. "It may be the only chance I'll ever get to use it."

Captain Smith did not return the smile. Commanding a ship was a serious business, and the decisions he would be called upon to make this night would be the most serious of a long and illustrious career. He turned to the sailor with the Morse lamp. "It's time, Harper. Fire the first rocket, and another every five or six minutes after that. We must attract the attention of that ship."

Mr. Isidor Straus, the owner of Macy's department store in New York City, took a step back from the lifeboat. "You go, my dear," he said to his wife. "The order is women and children. I'll follow in a little while."

"I'm sure," said First Officer Murdoch, "that there would be no objection if an elderly gentleman like yourself went aboard."

The multimillionaire was adamant. "I will not board ahead of the other men."

His wife retreated from the rail and took her husband's hand. "We've been together a long time," she said quietly. "Where you go, I go."

And the couple withdrew from the line.

Murdoch swallowed a lump in his throat. He knew only too well what the Strauses' decision might mean. He had been in command when the *Titanic* had struck the iceberg. The thought that the accident might have been avoided was almost too much for him to bear.

"Are there any more women and children?" he called. He reached out his arm to the next passenger. It was Amelia Bronson.

"Absolutely not!"

Murdoch was taken aback. "I beg your pardon?"

"Mother?" added Sophie.

"I refuse to take a seat in a lifeboat on the basis of 'women and children first!'"

"But, madam," Murdoch protested, "that has been the law of the sea for centuries!"

"Then it has been wrong for centuries," Mrs. Bronson said stubbornly. "I have devoted my life to the struggle for equality between women and men."

"Mother!" Sophie cried in alarm. "This has nothing to do with voting!"

"On the contrary, Sophie, it is exactly the same thing!" Her voice grew loud and strident, and she turned to face the passengers milling about the boat deck as if addressing one of her suffrage rallies. "Children require special treatment. We women do not. We are equal to men in intelligence, and must share in the decisions that shape our future. And we must share in the consequences when our endeavors go badly. It is demeaning for us to be coddled. I am just as capable of looking after myself as Mr. Straus."

"Then step aside, madam," Murdoch ordered. The first officer took the arm of the next woman in line, and helped her over the gunwale of the lifeboat.

Sophie turned furious eyes on her mother, and spoke as she had never done before. "I respect you and what you're trying to do for women, but this time you've gone too far!"

"On the contrary, I have not gone far enough. To effect great change, one must seize the opportunity of great moments. And what could be more momentous than this?"

"*Momentous?*" Sophie cried. "Have you lost your mind? How many votes will you cast from the bottom of the ocean?"

"Don't be so dramatic," her mother retorted. "I hardly think the ship is sinking."

"Well, think again. When they hold a lifeboat drill, they don't fill the boats, lower them, and set people adrift in the dead of night. I've seen the water filling up the lower decks. What would it take to convince you?"

At that very instant, there was a loud bang, followed by a whistling sound. All eyes looked to the sky as a white distress rocket burst above them, showering down a spray of shimmering stars.

It cast an eerie glow over the upturned faces.

CHAPTER SEVEN

RMS *CALIFORNIAN* —
MONDAY, APRIL 15, 1912, 12:45 A.M.

There was nothing quite as dreary as the overnight watch on a ship stopped dead in an ice field. Apprentice James Gibson had been watching the large steamer several miles distant, mostly because there was little else to do. She had come from the east at high speed, but it seemed as if she had barely moved for the past hour. Probably surrounded by ice, as the *Californian* was. Through his binoculars, he could make out the glow of lights on her deck.

"Like a circus parade," he murmured to himself, a little resentfully. Those luxury liners were like Christmas every day, one big party that never stopped. Now they were shooting off fireworks — at nearly one o'clock in the morning! The overprivileged wastrels! And irresponsible, too! What if someone mistook those skyrockets for — distress flares?

An icy hand clutched at his heart, and he reached

for the speaking tube that led down to Captain Lord's quarters. It was then he recalled the captain's exact words as he retired for the night: *I don't want to be disturbed unless the pack ice has closed around the ship and is crushing the hull.*

It couldn't be clearer than that.

Yet when he spied another rocket a few minutes later, he alerted Third Officer Groves, who was not quite so intimidated by Captain Lord.

Groves did not hesitate to pick up the speaking tube.

"Are they company signals?" came Lord's drowsy voice.

"White rockets, sir," Grove replied.

The captain's yawn clearly carried over the tube. "Try to reach them by Morse lamp. Keep me informed."

And the captain of the *Californian* went back to sleep.

☆

Alfie stumbled aft along Scotland Road, sloshing through ankle-deep water. He wept openly now, eyes blinded, oblivious to his surroundings. Not even when his mother had deserted him had he felt such utterly crushing loneliness. Somehow he had taken comfort in the fact that she was out there somewhere, alive — maybe even happy. But now there was no question that he had laid eyes on his father for the very last time. John Huggins had spent his life in the gritty heat of ships' boiler rooms, so perhaps it was fitting that the largest of them all would prove to be his tomb. But it still hurt. Oh, how it hurt!

The attack caught him completely by surprise. Hard wood struck him across the face, laying open his cheek, driving him backward so that he landed flat on the soggy deck, face bleeding. The shadowy figure that loomed over him, bludgeon raised to strike again, was something straight out of one of his mother's penny dreadfuls.

Mr. Masterson. Jack the Ripper himself.

Horror jolted Alfie out of his grief into sudden frantic action. He rolled to his left, a split second before the crutch came down again, splintering as it struck the deck. Masterson's legs were severely crippled, but living with his handicap had given him remarkable upper body strength.

"You may have found my scrapbook and learned my secret, but the book is fish food by now, and soon you will be, too. When rescue comes, I'll not have you spoiling my new life in America."

Alfie crab-walked in retreat, staying just out of the killer's reach. "We're all fish food!" he panted. "The ship's sinking by the head, and there aren't enough lifeboat berths for everyone!"

Masterson's smile was pure evil. "Not for you, perhaps. But a poor old cripple is surely an exception to 'women and children first.'"

By God, he's right. The realization was almost as jarring as the original blow with the crutch. Not even a living, breathing rule book like Lightoller would deny a lame man a place in a lifeboat. So the beast would survive, with all evidence of his crimes hidden forever at the bottom of the sea. He'd get his operation, his cure. And no one alive would be able to warn the people of New York of the danger that had landed on their shores.

Suddenly, Alfie lashed out both feet, sweeping the wasted legs from under Mr. Masterson. The older man went down like a stone. There was a sickening whack as his head struck the deck. The crutch dropped from his limp hand. Alfie raced to pick it up, raising it high, intending to stave in Masterson's skull and end the long unsolved nightmare of Jack the Ripper, once and for all.

He hesitated. Masterson was unconscious, but breathing. Alfie could see the fabric of his life belt rising and falling slightly with the movement of his chest. The ocean would surely do the rest. But just in case . . .

He sloshed forward along Scotland Road, and dropped the crutch down into the swirling water at the bottom of a work ladder. Now, even if the murderer regained consciousness, he would surely never make it up to the boat deck.

Icy water began to pool around Jack the Ripper, but he did not stir.

Paddy raced down the third-class staircase and froze at the bottom. Where was everybody? Not long before, most of steerage, a group hundreds strong, had milled around this spot, waiting to be summoned to the top deck. Perhaps they were being loaded onto boats at this very moment. But Paddy doubted it. Although he was no sailor or mathematician, good sense had told him that, when all the boats were loaded and gone, there would still be plenty of people left to go down with the mighty *Titanic*. And much of that unfortunate lot, he was willing to wager, would not be from first class.

But if they were on their way up top, Paddy could only imagine the long, complex path they must have been following. Since the last time he'd come down here, the gates to the aft well deck had been locked. What if other accesses were barred as well? Who knew how many people were lost in the maze of this vast ship? And *lost* meant *doomed*.

A high-pitched whimper reached his ears. He looked around. A dog? A cat? There were pets on the *Titanic*, but not in steerage. Third class generally had enough trouble feeding themselves. There was no extra money for animal food.

And then a small bundle of rags on a wooden bench sat up and began to cry.

Paddy's heart was wrung. This group must have departed in a state of panic, for someone had left a child behind. He went and sat beside the little girl.

"There now, you're all right. What's your name, then?"

The child was too terrified to speak, or perhaps too young. She could have been no more than two or three.

"Well, never mind. We'll go find your mum." He picked her up, and was warmed by the way she snuggled trustingly into his arms. She was light as a feather.

With the well deck closed off, Paddy had no choice but to head forward along E, marveling at the downhill angle. He and the child were nearly bowled over by rolling potatoes from an open storage room. The passageway jogged around the huge engine casing, and fed into the long corridor of Scotland Road. There Paddy narrowly missed a collision with a scrambling figure.

"Alfie!" he exclaimed. "You look like you've been in a right donnybrook!"

Alfie grimaced, causing the gash in his cheek to bleed even more. "You should see the other fellow," he panted. He stared at the child in Paddy's arms. "Is there anything you'd like to tell me?"

Paddy flushed. "She's not mine, of course! I found her at the base of the third-class staircase. Some poor family is due for a shock when they count heads. What are you doing here?"

Alfie's expression darkened further. "I said good-bye to my da."

Paddy digested this soberly. "I'm sorry, Alfie. But maybe he'll make it."

The young steward shook his head. "He's not even going to try."

There was a creaking sound, followed by a loud crack, and the pantry door burst open. A flood of biscuits, swollen with seawater, washed down the passageway. Frightened by the noise, the little girl began to weep again.

"Let's get this wee one on a lifeboat," said Paddy urgently.

They ascended to first class on a steep work stair, and made their way to the bedlam of the boat deck. It was twice as crowded as before, and politeness and decorum had fallen by the wayside. More than half of the boats had already been launched, and were rowing off far below on the glassy calm sea. Large clusters of anxious people surrounded the ones that remained. Passengers nearest to the rail could clearly see that the bow had sunk so low that the forward well deck was barely above the surface. Sinking — a joke bare minutes before — was becoming an inescapable reality.

The din was a mixture of shouted crew instructions and tearful good-byes between couples as the wives were helped into the lifeboats, leaving their husbands still aboard.

The men were cheery and optimistic:

"See you soon, my love."

"I'll just wait for the next boat."

"Look after the children. I'll be with you in a few hours."

Yet each passing moment made these assurances a little more anxious and strained as it became obvious that the *Titanic* would run out of lifeboats long before she ran out of passengers. Only the music remained upbeat. Through it all, ragtime rhythms bounced.

"Are they barmy, or just feeble-minded?" Paddy wondered, hefting the child. "Why would they keep playing *now*?"

Alfie shrugged miserably. "Why's Da still on his pump?" He looked around. "Which boat should we put her on?"

"Anywhere Lightoller isn't," Paddy said immediately. "Such a tiny thing, she is. It won't be hard to find space for her."

"Alfie! Paddy!"

They barely recognized Juliana, although they had seen her not half an hour before. Her face was tear-streaked, her eyes wide and bright red from crying. Her hair was unpinned, and hung loose and wet about her shoulders.

"Why aren't you on a boat?" Alfie demanded.

"Papa won't leave!" she sobbed. "He's playing cards! And he's winning!"

"He'll have no place to be spending that money," Paddy put in grimly. He had very little sympathy for the seventeenth Earl of Glamford, who was a poor father to his young daughter. Juliana's voyage to America had turned out to be for the purpose of betrothing her to the son of a wealthy Texas family, all to finance the earl's gambling debts and expensive lifestyle.

"That's not it," said Alfie, trying to be comforting. "He knows he has no chance at a lifeboat berth when it's women and children only. You have to let him do this his own way."

"By letting him *die*?" she shrilled.

"There's plenty of dying to be done around here tonight," Paddy predicted darkly. "It won't help his lordship if you're part of it." He thrust the whimpering child into her arms. "And you can take *her* while you're at it."

Juliana was thunderstruck as she wrapped her arms around the squirming bundle. "Who is she? Where is her family?"

"We'll have to sort that out later," Alfie decided.

"Her mother must be frantic!" Juliana insisted. "We must seek her out!"

The three faced the mob scene on the boat deck, hundreds strong and growing more crowded and chaotic as the seconds ticked away.

Chief Officer Wilde's voice rose above the hubbub. "Are there any more women and children?"

"Right here!" Alfie took Juliana's arm and began to push through the throng of men that now surrounded the chief officer.

The group refused to yield. If there were no more women, perhaps this was their turn at last — their chance at life. Paddy joined the shoving. In his months as a Belfast pickpocket, he had become adept at maneuvering through tight crowds.

"Very well — lower away," ordered Wilde. The lifeboat rocked with sudden movement.

"Wait!" bellowed Alfie, struggling helplessly.

CHAPTER EIGHT

Paddy reared back his leg and slammed a hobnail boot into the nearest shin. There was a cry of pain. A body gave way, and yet another. Paddy and Alfie bullied their way to the front, pushing Juliana and the child ahead of them.

"Two more!" Alfie shouted and stood firm as Juliana and her tiny charge were lifted over the gunwale. The last sight they had of her was through the struts of the rail.

Her face was white, her eyes huge and staring. "For God's sake, save yourselves!" she wailed.

Neither had a reply. But as she descended from view, Alfie turned to his friend. "I don't suppose you have a suggestion on how we're meant to accomplish that."

But Paddy had caught sight of a familiar figure in a tailored greatcoat and no life belt. "I'll be right back," he told Alfie. "There's something important I have to take care of."

Alfie stared. "Something important? More important than this?"

"I've a message to deliver," Paddy explained, "and I have a feeling this will be my last opportunity." He worked his way in from the side and fell into step behind the object of his attention.

Mr. Thomas Andrews, designer of the *Titanic*, moved with tireless energy about the boat deck. He did not seem to be rushing, and yet he got around very quickly, taking huge steps. One moment he was down on a knee, explaining to a sailor the best technique to pay out rope while lowering a lifeboat. The next, he was helping a frightened third-class woman fasten her life belt. And just as abruptly, he was conferring with J. Bruce Ismay, Managing Director of the White Star Line. If the designer was distraught over the impending fate of his masterpiece, he gave no sign.

Paddy followed him down a companion stair to A Deck and into the *Titanic*'s superstructure. The great man trod the magnificent corridor, peering into doorways in search of stragglers or anyone in need of assistance.

Paddy spoke up. "I'm told there are still card players in the lounge, sir. No ladies."

Andrews turned around, and regarded him in growing recognition. "I know you, do I not? You were the boy escaping the heat of the boiler rooms."

Paddy nodded. "Patrick Burns, sir. But we first met back at the shipyard in Belfast. I was with my friend Daniel Sullivan, who wanted to be an engineer like you."

Andrews nodded slowly. "The street lads. I remember." He frowned. "And since you are here, I deduce that you are the stowaway I've heard so much about. I'm afraid you've chosen a very unfortunate vessel for that enterprise. Is your friend Daniel aboard with you?"

"Daniel's dead," said Paddy bleakly. "We were on our way to give you something when he was murdered by the Gilhooleys."

"I'm sorry to hear it," Mr. Andrews said sincerely. "He was a clever lad. I recall he was very keen to show me a way the *Titanic* might sink." He laughed ruefully. "Apparently, fate has beaten him to it."

Paddy reached inside his shirt and took out a dog-eared, multifolded piece of paper. He had carried this with him, next to his heart, ever since the day of Daniel's murder. This was the diagram his friend had slaved over, the one that would prove there was no such thing as unsinkable. Paddy didn't understand any of it. But here at last he stood before the person who would — the man for whom it had been created in the first place.

He unfolded it carefully, and handed it over. "Was he right?"

Andrews studied the drawing for several long moments, his complexion fading to an unhealthy shade of gray. "By God!" he exclaimed, and repeated it more quietly. "By God. The boy had probably never even been to school, yet he was able to see what a trained engineer missed entirely!"

Paddy smiled in spite of himself. "Daniel was smart, he was," he said proudly. "I told you that in Belfast."

Andrews smoothed out the paper on a cocktail table. "See here," he explained. "Your friend could not have foreseen the iceberg. But he did predict — accurately, I'm afraid — that the greatest damage would be inflicted not by a head-on collision, but by a glancing blow along the side. Such a sideswipe would tear open a great many watertight compartments instead of just one or two. Would that I had seen this brilliant piece of work before the *Titanic* set sail."

"And if you had?" Paddy prompted. "Would you have canceled the maiden voyage?"

"I cannot say." The designer shook his head sadly. "Most likely the decision would not have been mine. The *Titanic* represents an investment of millions of pounds for the White Star Line, the largest and most expensive moving object ever assembled."

Paddy looked around at the opulent surroundings, marveling once again at the unsurpassed luxury of the doomed ship. "It didn't help, all those millions," he observed.

Andrews regarded him sadly. "Agreed. When the Atlantic closes over the top of my beautiful *Titanic*, it will not matter that her walls were rosewood paneled, her upholstery glove leather, and her chandeliers crystal." He regarded the stowaway with respect. "You are perhaps as wise as your unfortunate friend. And as unfortunate."

"Is there really nothing that can be done, Mr. Andrews?" Paddy persisted. "You know this ship better than anyone. Are we really all dead men?"

Andrews spoke very slowly and deliberately, as if trying to burn his words into Paddy's memory. "Don't wait for the ship to take you down, Patrick. When the sea is level with the deck, you must swim for it. There will be boats close by. You will have very little time to reach one of them. The water will be unbearably cold, enough to render you unconscious in minutes. If that happens, you will die."

Paddy swallowed hard. "Is that what you'll be doing, Mr. Andrews?"

Andrews smiled in resignation. "I was with the *Titanic* from the first rivet, and I'll be with her the rest of the way. I owe her that much."

Paddy didn't need to ask what that meant. The famous Thomas Andrews intended to go down with his ship.

CHAPTER NINE

RMS *CARPATHIA* —
MONDAY, APRIL 15, 1912, 1:45 A.M.

Captain Arthur Rostron had been at sea for twenty-seven years, yet never before had he given so many orders in so short a time. Plot a new course to the foundering *Titanic*. Cut off heat and hot water to divert all steam to the engines for maximum speed. Swing out lifeboats. Open gangway doors. Deploy rope ladders. Prepare hot food. Set up first aid stations in the dining saloons. Convert all extra space into quarters for the rescued.

Rostron's mind worked furiously. Had he thought of everything?

A dark curly head inserted itself into the captain's line of vision, and a young, accented voice said, "Almost eighteen knots. This is good speed, yes?"

Rostron's head whipped around. "What is this boy doing on my bridge?"

Cottam, the wireless operator, spoke up. "This is the lad I was telling you about, sir. Ambassador Curcovic's son. Drazen was on the wireless set when the C-Q-D from the *Titanic* came in."

"Well, then it would seem that we all owe you a debt of gratitude, Drazen," Rostron acknowledged.

"Will we get there on time, Captain?" the boy asked.

"We'd better hope so," Rostron replied, "or else we are brewing coffee when we should be preparing funeral shrouds."

☆

Juliana wasn't sure who was more frightened, the sobbing child or herself. The descent was like dropping off the edge of the earth into a featureless black abyss. They went down in rough, jarring jerks, often out of balance if the bow fell faster than the stern, or vice versa. The sway was such that, at times, it felt they would all be tipped out into the sea. She was sure she would have fallen except for the fact that the passengers were jammed in so tightly that no one could be dislodged from the pack. A small mercy, perhaps, but an important one.

A crewman near the bow shouted, "We are just over the condenser exhaust!"

"What's the condenser exhaust?" Juliana cried, and heard her question echoed by several others on board.

The answer came soon enough. She looked over the gunwale and saw a mighty flow of water shooting out of the hull of the *Titanic* under great pressure.

"We'll be swamped!" Juliana exclaimed.

And then they were in it. The stream struck their bow, and they were bounced and tossed like a badminton birdie, still suspended by the ropes from above.

All at once, the lights of the great ship were blocked by a long dark shape above them, coming down fast.

"It's another boat!" an elderly woman screamed.

Horror came with understanding. The condenser exhaust was pushing them into the path of the next descending lifeboat. If it landed on top of them, both would surely sink.

Sixty-four passengers and crew all began yelling at the same instant. "*Sto-o-op!*"

But the boat deck was many stories above them, and there was no chance of their being heard in the urgency and disorder of the moment.

"Look under your feet!" ordered the crewman at the bow. "There's a pin that frees us from the ropes!"

But in all the panic, no one could seem to find any-thing.

Passengers and crewmen were on their feet, hack-ing at the thick lines with knives, sewing scissors, even hairpins. The descending hull was just a few feet above them now, blotting out everything but their dread. Juliana eased the child to the deck, and hunched over her — although what protection would her slim frame be if they were all crushed?

And then the last strand of rope was severed, and the force of the condenser exhaust sent them bounc-ing over white water away from the *Titanic*. The other craft hit the surface where Juliana's lifeboat had been a split second before.

She reached down and picked up the little girl amid terror and relief all around them.

"You see, poppet? There was never anything to be afraid of!"

When the last shimmering rocket faded to nothing and winked out in the sky, Captain Smith found him-self in a situation unique in his long and illustrious career. He had nothing to do. It was not yet time to release his crew from their duties and declare every man for himself. Aside from that, only one obligation remained to him — to go down with his ship as sea captains had done since the first primitive raft had been set afloat by the ancients.

But right now, he stood idle as his officers proceeded with the loading of what few boats remained, and the Marconi operators continued to transmit the distress calls C.Q.D. and S.O.S. Several ships were on their way, coming hard, but even the closest of them, the *Carpathia*, was fifty-eight miles away. At the moment the *Titanic* foundered, her passengers and crew would be on their own. In these icy waters, massive loss of life was inescapable.

And he, their captain, could do nothing to prevent it. The feeling of helplessness was also foreign to him. And much more painful. He could not keep his mind from reliving every moment of the voyage. Was there something he could have done to prevent this disaster? What if he had resisted Mr. Ismay's call to light the last two boilers? The managing director of the White Star Line had envisioned only headlines of a triumphant early arrival in New York. But while Ismay was his employer, it was the captain who had final authority once the voyage was under way. Would that reduced speed have given the *Titanic* the precious time to port around the iceberg?

He grimaced. Mr. Ismay would have his headlines, all right, but not quite the ones he'd expected.

A stellar career of spotless decisions — right up until the last one. Perhaps history would forgive E. J. Smith. He would never forgive himself.

Some ten miles distant, the lights of that ship still winked, taunting him. By heaven, they had to be all blind not to have seen his rockets! Blind or criminally indifferent! The master of that vessel was every bit as responsible for what was to come as Smith himself.

He looked aft at the activity beyond the bridge. The boat deck was packed with desperate and anxious people. The *Titanic*'s fate was no longer a mystery, even to the rankest landlubber. The forward well deck was gone now, the forepeak poking out of the ocean like a triangular island, the mast and crow's nest at a dizzying angle. The pitch of the deck was becoming more unforgiving as the bow dipped and the stern rose. But most unforgiving of all was the cruel arithmetic of lifeboat berths. Only two boats remained to be filled, plus two of the smaller Engelhardt collapsibles that the crew was laboring to free from the roofs of the wheelhouse and officers' quarters.

Sweeping the ranks of the doomed, his eyes fell on two women standing apart from the others, animated by what looked like a heated argument. It was that American suffragist, Mrs. Bronson, and her young daughter. Why on earth were two first-class ladies still aboard?

He straightened his sagging shoulders. Here was something he could turn his hand to — saving the lives of two of his passengers, even if he could not save them all.

He joined them by the lattice frame that protected the dome of the grand staircase, and wasted no time on pleasantries. "Ladies, come with me at once. There is no time to lose."

Amelia Bronson balked. "I categorically refuse to take a man's place in a lifeboat simply because I am female."

"Madam, do you see a newspaper reporter any-where about who will tell the world of your brave but futile gesture? Even if such a person were here, he would be lost, and his notebook with him. The headlines you seek will never be published. You are dooming not just yourself but your young daughter, and all for naught."

"Take Sophie! She'll survive and tell my story!"

"I will *not*!" Sophie seethed. "If you do this to me, Mother, I'll make it my mission to ensure that no one ever hears how anxious you were to throw your life away for nothing!"

Her mother was adamant. "How would it look to

the world if Amelia Bronson were to be plucked out
of the ocean alive because she used her gender to gain
a lifeboat berth ahead of elderly and infirm men —
perhaps even a cripple like that man Masterson?"

"*Masterson?!*" Sophie exclaimed. "Save your sympathy for someone worthy of it! Do you know who
that monster is? He's Jack the Ripper, that's who!"

The captain spoke harshly to Mrs. Bronson. "Your
obstinate behavior is causing your daughter to lose
touch with reality. Jack the Ripper, indeed!"

"All right, I'll do it!" Sophie exclaimed suddenly.
"I'll get on the boat! I'll tell everybody how you sacri-
ficed yourself for the cause! But at least come with
me now so we can say our last good-byes!"

"Mr. Lightoller is loading Boat 4 from the A Deck
promenade, port side," the captain said briskly.
"Good luck."

Arm in arm, the Bronson women descended to
A Deck.

"I understand how difficult this is for you," Amelia
said soothingly to her daughter. "Thank you for realizing why I have no choice but to do this."

"You're welcome." Considering that she was about
to say a final farewell to her mother, Sophie would
not look Amelia in the eye.

"And you'll have to explain this to your father,"

Mrs. Bronson went on. "But of course he'll understand. After twenty-two years of marriage, he knows me."

They could already see the crowd gathered on the enclosed promenade. A window had been opened, and the boat dangled outside. Lightoller balanced on the sill, helping women over the gunwale. As the Bronsons joined the group, Sophie reflected that, at any other time, she would have been impressed by the cross section of American East Coast high society that was represented here — names like Astor, Thayer, Ryerson, and Carter.

Chairs had been set up to serve as steps to the high windowsill. On one of these perched Colonel Astor himself, helping his young wife into Boat 4. When she was established in a seat, the renowned tycoon faced Mr. Lightoller.

"May I accompany her, sir? She is in a delicate condition."

The second officer never changed expression. "No men are allowed until all the women are aboard, sir."

Colonel Astor stepped back without a word of argument. The multimillionaires all stood by as their wives and families were loaded one by one onto the craft that would take them to safety. There were tears and tender partings, but the mood was dignified and subdued.

From his perch on the sill, Lightoller spotted the Bronsons, and motioned them forward.

"I'll not be going," the suffragist informed the second officer. "But please put my daughter in the boat."

Sophie stepped up on the chair, holding on to her mother for dear life. "Hug me, Mother, one last time! I'm so scared!"

"Be strong, my darling girl!" Mrs. Bronson climbed up onto the chair, and took her daughter into her arms.

Sophie's reaction was deliberate and lightning-fast. She wrapped one arm around her mother, threw out a slender hip, and used Amelia's own momentum to propel her over the sill and out the window. There were cries of shock as the suffragist tumbled over the gunwale and into the crowded craft.

CHAPTER TEN

RMS *TITANIC* —
MONDAY, APRIL 15, 1912, 2:00 A.M.

Lightoller nodded at Sophie in wide-eyed respect. "That, miss, might be the finest action any of us will see this night!" He held out an arm to hand her through the window, but a call came from the crewman manning the boat:

"We're full up, Mr. Lightoller. Lower away."

Lightoller gave the order, and then turned to Sophie. "We'll have to find you another place. Come with me."

The screams that came from Amelia Bronson were barely human.

"It's all right, Mother!" Sophie tried to call down. "There's another boat! I'll see you soon!" She doubted her mother could hear her over her own wailing.

Sophie brushed past the world's wealthiest people and followed Lightoller back up to the boat deck. All around, ropes dangled from empty davits. And, on the forward-most port side, the last lifeboat was just being lowered.

"Stop!" shouted Lightoller, and rushed over, towing Sophie by the arm. "I have one more!"

They looked down into the wooden craft. It was full, even overloaded. There was not an inch to spare. Lightoller didn't say it. There was nothing to say. Sophie had saved her mother's life, but it seemed that it would be at the cost of her own.

A large, round face with muttonchop whiskers looked up from the descending boat. "Cease and desist!" bellowed the familiar voice of Major Mountjoy. "I yield my place to that young lady! Raise us back at once!" His cries did not reach the sailors operating the falls, and the lifeboat continued to descend. In great distress, the major stood up and tried to climb back aboard the *Titanic*. His great weight threw the craft out of balance. It swung away from the hull, and came back with a jolt. Two men stood up and jammed the major into his seat. Sophie could not make out their words, but it was plain that they were yelling at him as the boat continued down.

In spite of her dire situation, a giggle escaped her. Even on a sinking ship, Major Muttonchop was the perfect clown.

If only Julie were here to see this!

She bit her lip. Thank goodness Juliana wasn't! She prayed that her friend had made it safely onto a boat.

She turned huge eyes on the second officer. "Is there any hope at all, Mr. Lightoller?"

"Stay with me," Lightoller ordered, pointing to the roof of the officers' quarters. There were two more Engelhardt collapsibles, and a small crowd of passengers and crew were struggling to release them from their moorings. Their distance from the davit made them almost impossible to launch, but Lightoller had another idea. "We might be able to float them away when the sea rolls over the bow."

Despite the chaos of the moment, Lightoller instantly assumed command of the group working on Collapsible B. The complicated tangle of ropes was cleared away, and the men fell into place to lift the boat off of the cabin roof. It was heavy and cumbersome, and the pitch of the deck made the operation even more difficult. Sophie ran over to lend her own strength to the task. It was like working uphill on the side of a mountain — she glanced sideways — and the mountain was about to be underwater. The forecastle was completely submerged now, with gentle waves lapping at the superstructure just a few feet below them. They would be swamped in a matter of minutes — if that long.

Lightoller bellowed, "Heave!" A mighty effort brought the craft clear of the roof. But the man beside Sophie lost his footing on the slope, upsetting the balance of the heavy boat. The Engelhardt tumbled off the cabin top, and crashed to the deck, upside down.

Sophie threw herself clear, narrowly missing having her leg crushed by the overturned gunwale. As she scrambled up again, her eyes focused on a slight crewman in baggy coveralls, laboring at the boat's peak.

She felt an irrational amount of joy at the sight of a familiar face. "*Paddy!*"

Lightoller knew all too well the name of the stowaway who had been evading him for so long. Everything else forgotten, he drew his pistol and aimed it at the boy.

Paddy's reaction was instantaneous. He hurled himself to the deck just as the second officer squeezed the trigger. The bullet whined over his head and buried itself in the base of the first smokestack.

"*No!*" Without thinking, Sophie attacked Lightoller. Shock rendered him momentarily helpless, and he held still as she beat him with tightly clenched fists.

"Can't you let him be?" she sobbed in fury. "We'll all be dead in a minute, anyway!" In the past hours, she had wrestled with Jack the Ripper and now this officer. Just then she would have been unable to decide which of them was the bigger villain.

Lightoller broke free from her and stood stock-still, a look of utter bewilderment on his face. It was the first time Sophie had ever seen anything other than decisive confidence on those harsh features — as if Charles Herbert Lightoller had never before encountered a situation that was not detailed in the manual of His Majesty's Merchant Service.

At that moment, with the parties posed as if frozen in time, the deck lurched sharply downward, throwing all of them off their feet. Yet before Sophie struck anything solid, the ocean came. It was not a wave so much as the sea filling in the space where the wheelhouse and officers' quarters had been seconds before.

And then they were well and truly in the water, swept off the *Titanic* along with the two collapsibles, one right side up, and Boat B still upside down.

Nothing could have prepared Sophie for the cold. It was the deep searing jab of a needle applied to every single inch of her body. She began to pant uncontrollably with the racing beat of her heart. From her fingertips to her toes, her muscles cramped painfully, paralyzing her. The water closed over her head, and panic set in. The adrenaline rush released her muscles from their prison, and the life belt buoyed her up. She broke the surface of the water in time to see people leaping from the sharply tilted boat deck, trying to get onto the two collapsibles. A lucky few made it aboard. Others bobbed in the black water, too stunned by the icy cold to try to save themselves. The agonized screams were terrifying to hear. She would surely have been screaming herself if she could have mustered the breath.

She tried to swim, frenzied thrashing strokes hampered by the bulky life belt and her sodden clothing. To her horror, the collapsibles were drifting farther away, propelled by the swell created by the sinking of the bow. Try as she might, she could not manage to cry for help.

So be it, she thought. The boats were her one chance at life. No one could last long in this water. She had to face the inescapable fact that survival was slipping away.

She stopped swimming and averted her gaze from the rescue that was not going to happen. There was a long, thick pole directly behind her, sticking out of the ocean at a forty-five-degree angle. Hallucination?

No! The foremast!

She kicked toward it with all the frenetic energy of a dying girl. Her eyes were clenched shut with effort when her head actually bumped into it. She clamped her arms around the wood, and dragged herself clear of the ocean's murderous clutches.

CHAPTER ELEVEN

Paddy was flat on the deck when the wave hit, more worried about the second officer's pistol than any danger posed by the sea. The cold knifed through him, and he began to swim by pure instinct, his arms and legs moving furiously in an attempt to generate some heat. He moved forward for a few seconds. But then an irresistible force dragged him under. Seawater was pouring into the ventilator at the base of the funnel, and he was being sucked downward. He windmilled his arms in a desperate attempt to fight the pull, but the force was overwhelming, and he continued to descend. Suddenly, he slammed into the grill at the top of the air shaft. It knocked out the breath he'd been holding, and he swallowed icy water, choking and tasting salt.

He struggled to free himself, but the suction was too strong, pinning him to the grating.

I'm drowning, he thought. But in reality, what he felt was the oxygen starvation from *not* drowning, from shutting down all respiration in an attempt to keep the water out. In the end, it didn't matter, for in either event, he would be dead, and soon.

Deep within the *Titanic*, a swamped boiler released a tremendous cloud of superheated steam. Paddy was aware of a rush of warmth, followed by a roiling maelstrom of bubbles. And then he was being blasted off the grating and propelled through the water like a torpedo. He broke the surface and wheezed in great gulps of frosty air. After the burn of the steam, he was almost grateful to be cold again.

When at last he dared to open his stinging eyes, he was amazed to find himself only a few feet from the overturned Collapsible B. The hull was draped with men, drenched, shivering, and moaning. Paddy splashed over and reached out a hand. "Help me!" he croaked.

A soggy shoe kicked out at him. "There's no help to be had here." The voice was not angry or cruel, just utterly, utterly exhausted.

"Sorry, boy, but we can't take you on," said another man, his mustache glittering with ice crystals. "You'll swamp the boat and kill us every one."

Paddy grabbed hold of a cleat. All he could do was bob there beside the Engelhardt, waiting for the frigid sea to sap what little life force remained in him.

☆

Alfie watched in stunned disbelief as the sea engulfed the wheelhouse and crew quarters, and rolled over the boat deck, hungry for more. In a series of thunderous crashes, the huge stained-glass dome over the Grand Staircase shattered under the weight of the water, and the Atlantic poured into the *Titanic*'s opulent heart.

Up until this point, the passengers left topside had remained fairly calm. They were calm no longer. The panic was total. More than fifteen hundred people remained on the sinking ship. The vast majority of them ran aft, a stampede that rattled the deck every bit as much as the swamping of the bow.

The crew stampeded right along with the passengers, their duties complete, released by their captain. A small number of them were tossing lounge chairs and furniture overboard — anything that might offer flotation to a swimmer.

Some people were actually jumping into the water, in the hope of being picked up by one of the lifeboats.

Or perhaps their plan was to swim as far away as possible to avoid being pulled under when the ship made its final plunge into the inky depths. Many might not have been thinking at all.

Afraid of being trampled, Alfie descended to A Deck and continued his escape along the enclosed promenade. Soon he was one of scores climbing down to the aft well deck. By now the stern had tipped up so high that one man literally walked along the wall like a fly. Up onto the poop deck they poured, hundreds of them, striving to reach the one place aboard the *Titanic* that seemed farthest from the terrible sea. There were no shouted instructions, no rational conversations. There were just screams. Every second the stern rose higher. The final twenty yards to the poop deck's rail were like the alpine ascent of a mountain.

Alfie looked down the length of the *Titanic*, all lights still blazing, and knew the end was very near.

Sophie, numb with exhaustion, shinnied higher and higher up the foremast, only to find the water no farther away. As the bow went down, the mast went with it. Yet she knew she had to hold on as long as possible. This perch, as awkward, cold, and miserable as it was, represented survival.

Every second you're in that water, you're dying.

Her one joy was that she had managed to save her mother, despite Amelia Bronson's best efforts to kill herself. At least Daddy would have somebody.

A loud ripping sound came from overhead as the giant front smokestack tore away from the ship and toppled over. With a gasp, Sophie squeezed her eyes shut and waited to be annihilated by a mass ten thousand times her weight. She felt a hot wind blow over her as it passed, tearing the mast rigging and dropping her into the sea. She hit the icy water a split second before the funnel did. It kicked up a wave that tossed her high in the air. When she came down again, she was caught in the eddy created by the sinking stack. The buoyancy of her life belt was powerless to counteract the relentless pull. Down went Sophie Bronson, deep below the surface.

☆

Viewed from a lifeboat, the sinking *Titanic* was a beautiful and terrifying sight. The sea was so calm, the night so black, that the ship glowed with an unearthly power. It was horrible to behold, and yet no one could look away.

Juliana had not stopped sobbing since they had rowed from the crippled vessel.

Her sole comfort was that the little one in her arms

had finally fallen asleep. The child would be spared this awful sight and the memory that would no doubt haunt all of them for the rest of their lives.

Slowly, the stern rose up until the ship was nearly vertical.

"Almost as tall as the Eiffel Tower," commented a woman in a hushed voice. "We saw it while in Paris. It was our honeymoon, you know...." Her voice broke.

"My father is aboard," Juliana barely whispered. And who else? Sophie? Alfie? Paddy? She felt guilty to be thinking only about her own circle. There had to be hundreds still on the ship — perhaps more than a thousand!

And then a low rumbling clamor traveled across the water from the doomed vessel, growing in intensity.

"Oh, my God!" a woman shrilled. "She's exploding!"

☆

At the tip of the stern, Alfie latched on to the railing, and held on like grim death as the very deck beneath his feet swung to an impossible angle. All around him, screaming people were sliding, skidding, falling. Some tried to jump into the water — from this height, surely a fatal drop. He had seen many sickening sights in the past few hours, including an attempted murder by Jack the Ripper himself. This was by far the most terrible.

As the slope steepened toward vertical, he felt his feet leaving the ship. The thought of hanging a hundred and fifty feet up terrified him. His hands were too cold, his strength too depleted, to maintain that grip. He hoisted himself up over the rail so that, when it became horizontal, he was lying on top of it.

He felt the sound before he heard it — a loud reverberating roar that seemed to emanate from the *Titanic*'s very core, like the great vessel protesting her fate. He remembered Da telling him that the colossal reciprocating engines and iron furnaces were not actually attached to the ship. Their weight alone held them in place. Now they were falling, crashing through bulkheads and compartments, eradicating everything in their path. The thought of John Huggins was a hammer blow to his son's chest. He would never know the actual moment of his father's death. But it was a certainty in the violent upheaval that was taking place in the bowels of the *Titanic* now.

As long as you see the lights, Da had said, *you'll know that's me.*

Those lights had shone without interruption throughout this ghastly night. Now they flickered once, then winked out forever. A discordant grinding screech rose above the din as the entire bow was rent from the ship, breaking her in two. Still clamped to the rail, Alfie was suddenly falling as the stern dropped from vertical to near horizontal. It bounced in the ocean, drenching him and nearly hurling him from his purchase. He was aware of horrible screams all around him as people were dislodged from the ship, raining down like autumn leaves in a gust of wind. Then he was soaring again, back to upright as the ocean rushed into the *Titanic*'s open hind-quarters. He hung there, shivering, trying to catch his breath, and wondering when the final descent would begin.

He did not have long to wait. With a deep rolling groan, the *Titanic* began her death plunge. The motion was so perfectly vertical that Alfie was able to scramble up, standing on the rounded steel plates of the stern itself, waiting to meet the sea. The feeling was not entirely different from riding down in one of the ship's lifts.

Astounded by his calm after the total hysteria of

the past few hours, he simply waited for the ocean to present itself, and stepped off into the water.

Inches behind him, with little more than a dignified burble, the most magnificent ship the world had ever known slipped beneath the waves and was seen no more.

CHAPTER TWELVE

LATITUDE 41° N, LONGITUDE 50° W —
MONDAY, APRIL 15, 1912, 2:20 A.M.

Alfie expected to be sucked down by the sinking ship; in actuality, he barely got his hair wet. The feeling of control disappeared the instant he was in the water. The cold was almost heat, as if he had been set on fire rather than submerged. A cry was torn from him, and he was shocked to realize that he could be making such a tortured sound. The same agonized wailing was coming from all around him, not loud or strident, but constant and penetrating. It rose from the ocean, melding into an eerie symphony of suffering.

Without warning, Alfie was driven under the water by a force pressing down on his shoulders. Choking on saltwater, he twisted to see a man of middle age holding on to him with desperate hands.

"Help me! Save me!"

Alfie sputtered to the surface. "Stop it! You'll drown us both!"

But the man was hysterical, teeth chattering from the cold. "I beg you!" He grabbed at Alfie again, wrapping one arm around the young steward's neck.

Wheezing, Alfie did the only rational thing. He pushed the man off with all his might. It was as the terrified face veered away from him that Alfie realized the poor soul was wearing no life belt. He sank like a stone, and never resurfaced.

Did I kill him? Or did I prevent him from killing me?

He could not bring his half-frozen mind to focus on the question. He could only swim. And pray.

The *Titanic*'s end was the most otherworldly thing Juliana had ever seen. One moment the largest moving object ever built by man, shining like the sun, towered over the North Atlantic. The next, she was gone as if she had never even been there, the sea glassy calm over the place where she'd sunk out of sight.

Across the water the night air carried the keening sound of souls crying out in torment.

The first reaction in Boat 13 was disbelief. "My

God!" exclaimed a woman, trying to hold her hands over her children's ears.

"It's the people in the water!" Juliana breathed in horror. "They're dying!"

"It sounds like hundreds of them!" someone added. "Why aren't they in lifeboats?"

"I wouldn't know, ma'am," said the crewman in command. "I'm just an assistant purser. I couldn't tell you how many boats there are — or how few."

"We must go back!" Juliana exclaimed suddenly. "We must pick up as many of those unfortunates as possible!"

The young crewman was surprised. "We're full to bursting, miss! We couldn't fit in so much as a tooth-pick without endangering ourselves!"

Juliana's voice rose along with the swell of the wailing sound. "These are our fathers, our brothers, our friends! Some of you have left husbands behind!"

"Not all the lifeboats are full up," offered a steerage lady. "Surely they'll try to help."

Juliana peered desperately out into the black velvet night. Where were the boats returning to pick up survivors?

Where?

☆

Alfie never stopped swimming, as if he believed he could make it back to England if he simply applied himself. The cold was beyond imagining. Nor was it anything a body became accustomed to. Each moment was more bone-chilling, more painful, more horrible than the one that had come before. It was a deterioration that could only end in death. He had already passed many unconscious and dead, and bumped into more than one. The experience of looking into the blue complexions and staring, lifeless eyes would be with him always, he knew.

For this reason, he was not shocked when he felt a jolt. But the object in front of him was much larger than a corpse, and hard to the touch. He squinted, straining for night sight when the only light came from stars. A huge piece of furniture bobbed there, dark wood, with shelving and small compartments. He grasped at a knob, and a drawer pulled out in his hand, spilling multicolored birthday candles into the black sea.

A pantry from one of the galleys! It must have been washed overboard when the *Titanic* split in two.

To this frozen, drowning boy it represented salvation.

It was not until he tried to haul himself on top of it

that he realized how much of his strength was gone. It took every ounce of his will to drag his sodden body onto the broad face of the massive kitchen unit. As he settled onto the shelving, he could hear a gurgling sound — seawater penetrating the compartments and cubbies.

No — I *will not sink twice,* he vowed, almost angry at the prospect of going down a second time. He began to pull out every drawer, every shelf, every hinged lid, jettisoning all excess weight. Canned goods, bags of flour, exotic spices, confectioner's sugar, wild rice — he dumped it all into the Atlantic. The one thing he saved was a glass jar of French bonbons. It would provide quick energy, and, if the worse came to the worst, a bailing bucket.

At last, he lay there, panting, soaking wet in the bitterly cold air, and actually felt warmer.

He lay semiconscious for a few moments, wondering about the wheeze he could hear deep in his chest. He was so far gone that, when he first heard the cries for help, he had almost forgotten where he was. Memory flooded back, and he knew one thing: If fate gave him the chance, he had to save as many people as humanly possible.

He couldn't see the figure in the water, but he could make out the splashing of flailing arms. "Over here!"

he croaked. With effort, he struggled up and reached out his hands to the floundering swimmer.

Alfie was surprised by the power in the grip that locked onto his wrists. The man heaved and groaned, and the pantry listed dangerously.

"Easy," Alfie urged. "You'll flip us."

The swimmer calmed his movements, squirming onto the wood of the cabinet. Alfie hauled him into the center, reestablished balance, and sat down, exhausted.

Utterly spent, his new passenger looked up and began to thank his rescuer.

Alfie stared in disbelief. It was Masterson.

Jack the Ripper.

The debilitating fatigue in Masterson's eyes vanished, to be replaced by blazing rage. Somehow, the cripple found strength in his all-but-useless legs and launched himself at Alfie. A powerful arm locked around Alfie's torso, dragging him toward the side of the makeshift raft. The pantry lurched, sloshing water over both of them.

Alfie retaliated, boxing the older man's ears with the heels of his hands. Masterson cried out, but squeezed harder. Breathless and desperate to break the suffocating grip, Alfie gouged at the man's eyes. With a bellow of fury, Masterson fell away. The storage cabinet heeled and took on another icy wave. Alfie scrambled up, his boots splashing in three inches of water. The pantry bobbed ever lower, losing buoyancy as the sea lapped in over the side.

"Stop it, you old fool!" Alfie barked. "You may kill me, but you're sinking yourself at the same time!"

"You'll not spoil my plans, boy!" Masterson brayed.

"Neither of us has need of plans if we capsize!"

Something in Alfie's words must have penetrated to the murderer's addled brain, because Masterson backed away slowly. Alfie, too, retreated from his enemy, moving carefully to keep the shaky craft in balance.

He knew that, at the first opportunity, this evil beast would be upon him again. Masterson could not let him live — not as long as Alfie knew his terrible secret. The one thing keeping the young steward alive was the flimsiness of their life raft. The killer could not kill without sealing his own fate. In this precarious position, any attack by either combatant would be murder-suicide.

I should do it, Alfie thought suddenly. *It would be a good trade. I could save New York from Jack the Ripper! Maybe it doesn't hurt so much to drown. . . .*

But he couldn't — not while there was still an

opportunity to be rescued. He felt a flush of shame. He was nobody, and he had no one now that Da was gone. But life — even a slim chance at it — was precious, and he lacked the courage to do what needed to be done.

Who knew how many young American women would be put in danger because of the cowardice of one English boy on this night of horror?

A truce with Jack the Ripper. A deal with the devil.

CHAPTER THIRTEEN

Paddy hung off the side of the overturned collapsible and wondered why he would even bother doing such a futile thing.

There must have been thirty men kneeling, sitting, and lying on the Engelhardt's bottom. There wasn't room for so much as a mouse, let alone a dying Irish boy.

It was just about the fate he deserved, he supposed, after his heedlessness had gotten Daniel killed. Well, he'd be joining his friend soon enough. The icy water that surrounded him almost up to his neck had made him so numb that he wasn't sure his legs were still there. The only feeling he had at all was in his hands, which clung desperately to a cleat on the Engelhardt. And what he felt was pain. No one could survive for long like this. The night was filled with the cries and moans of fifteen hundred people floating in their life belts, yet with each passing minute, the chorus of agony grew quieter, the multitude of voices dwindling.

They're dying. And me with them.

What possible purpose could be served by this kind of torture? To prolong the suffering for a few more minutes?

Or I could just let go.

Paddy had been living on borrowed time ever since he'd set out on foot from his home in County Antrim for the cruel streets of Belfast. Well, now that debt was being called in. It seemed only fair.

When the force struck him from above, it detached him from the boat, driving him underwater. The buoyancy of his life belt brought him back to the surface, and he found himself bobbing next to the man with the mustache who had denied him space on the upturned boat. The poor soul was stiff and staring, stone dead of exposure.

The sudden drenching of his head seemed to restore the function of his brain. One dead man gone meant there was an empty space aboard. Paddy didn't cherish the idea of taking advantage of another person's misfortune.

But if one more can be saved, it might as well be me.

A moment before he'd had no energy left. Now he was scrambling, climbing, heaving himself onto the convex hull. It was so crowded that he was crawling across men's legs, but no one complained. No one had the strength.

He found his place, not by any choice, but at the moment when he could make it no farther. It was too crowded for him to collapse, so he just settled there, like a jellyfish, wedged between two bodies.

"Keep still," came a sharp order from the man on his left. "It wouldn't take much to upset this applecart."

Even in Paddy's depleted state, he could not help but recognize that voice. He looked up in dismay into the stern, unyielding countenance of Mr. Lightoller.

Lightoller's eyes narrowed in recognition. "You!"

Instinctively, Paddy glanced at the man's hands and then pockets, searching for the second officer's gun. It was nowhere in sight and, even if Lightoller still had it, it was surely too wet to fire. But, Paddy realized, the simple act of throwing his hated stowaway overboard would be as lethal as a bullet to the head.

"Well, you did it, sir," Paddy croaked. "You got me off your precious *Titanic*. I hope you're happy now."

Lightoller stared at him in disbelief for a long moment, then nodded brusquely. "You're not a stowaway anymore, boy. The *Titanic* is gone, and you've as much right to your life as any of us. Besides, you're lucky, and we have need of that this night. Tell whatever angel is looking out for you to send a ship, and very soon, or there won't be anyone to rescue but corpses."

Paddy's teeth chattered. If this was luck, he pitied the poor fool who was *un*lucky.

Sophie had been swimming forever, certain that frantic activity was the sole thing keeping her alive in the frigid water. She had watched from across the glassy smooth sea as the mighty *Titanic* had broken in half like a child's toy and disappeared beneath the waves. She had struggled among the dead and dying, closing her mind to a horror that was beyond comprehension, and yet all too real. To think was to die. Only in constant motion was there any chance for survival. But the lifeboats were so far away, and moving even farther. Why weren't they coming back? Didn't they hear the howls of the people in the water?

So focused was she on the distant boats that she almost missed the wooden object directly ahead. What was it? It wasn't a boat. And the *Titanic* didn't have flat life rafts, did it? She made up her mind. Whatever it was, it was floating. And that was good enough for her.

It had seemed to Sophie that she'd been swimming with strength and vigor. She now realized that had been an illusion. The floating object was no more than forty feet away, yet it was taking her an awfully long time to get there. The strokes that had felt so powerful were little more than the pitiful flailing of an exhausted girl.

She was right upon it, close enough to touch it. At last, her hand felt something solid, and she grasped the wood with nerveless fingers, knowing that she might never muster the force it would take to climb on top of it. And suddenly, a figure was looming over the edge, reaching for her.

"Thank you!" she tried to say, but the sound didn't travel any farther than her own ears.

And then the hands, rather than bringing her

aboard, closed around her throat. An iron grip began to squeeze.

She already knew who her attacker was — who else would try to commit a murder *now,* in the midst of this gargantuan tragedy?

She looked up through the darkness into the mad eyes of Jack the Ripper.

She found her voice then, uttering a piercing shriek that sliced through the night.

The grip tightened, cutting off her cry. She gasped for breath, and there was none. Sophie, who had avoided drowning, would suffocate nonetheless at the hands of a ravening beast.

She tried with her entire being to break his hold on her, digging her fingernails into his hands. It was no use. His strength was too great, and hers was all but gone. The stars over the horizon blurred as her consciousness began to fall away.

A heavy jar swung out over Masterson, shattering against the back of his head. Bonbons and glass shards rained down onto Sophie. The vise around her throat relaxed, and Masterson fell forward, unconscious, his face hanging over the side in the water.

Another figure bent over her.

"Alfie!" she rasped. She had never in her life been so happy to see anyone.

"Don't talk, Miss Sophie. Save your strength." He grasped her under her arms and tried to haul her aboard the floating pantry.

Sophie realized that he was almost as weak as she was, and that she would have to help if she were ever to get out of the water. Somehow, she managed to fling one leg over the side, and then roll until she was on the pantry and lying flat. She was so completely spent, so cold, that she almost forgot the man who had been trying to kill her for the second time that night.

With great effort, she raised herself up on her elbow. Masterson was still unconscious, his head trailing in the black water. He was most certainly drowned.

"Is he — ?" she began.

Alfie nodded. "I think so. I don't cheer the death of any man, but in his case I can make an exception."

Sophie shuddered. "Get him away, Alfie. I can't look at him. Just the thought of the horrible things he's done —"

Alfie leaned over and began to unfasten Masterson's life belt. "When I was little, my mother used to tell me about him. She said, 'I'll never sleep soundly in

my bed until that monster is off the streets for good.'"
He tossed the belt aside, and pushed the body overboard, watching as Jack the Ripper splashed into the
black water and sank out of sight.

"Sleep well, Mum."

CHAPTER FOURTEEN

RMS *CARPATHIA* —
MONDAY, APRIL 15, 1912, 2:45 A.M.

The wireless shack was unbearably cold.

All the *Carpathia* was cold, and calls were coming in from shivering passengers. With full power to the engines, and the ship steaming north, the temperature in their cabins had dropped twenty degrees.

"Is there any word?" asked Drazen anxiously.

Marconi Officer Cottam wore the headset, his expression growing grimmer by the moment. They had not heard from the sinking *Titanic* in almost an hour. Then the message had been: *Come as quickly as possible, old man. The engine room is filling up to the boilers.*

"Nothing," was the reply. "Of course, if the boilers are swamped, there's no steam for the dynamos. No power, no wireless."

Drazen nodded soberly. He didn't believe it, either. "Are there any other ships coming?"

"Yes, but we're the closest. And we're still at least an hour away."

Drazen shuddered. He was afraid there would be very little left of the *Titanic* by the time the *Carpathia* got there. "How long can people survive in the water?"

"*That* water?" Cottam was technically an employee of the Marconi company, and not a sailor. But he had worked in transatlantic shipping long enough to understand the lethal cold of the northern route. Only the salt and constant motion kept the sea from freezing solid. "Minutes. Maybe less."

Chief Steward Harry Hughes appeared in the doorway of the wireless shack. "Captain Rostron wants to see the boy."

Drazen goggled. "*Me?* Why?"

"I don't question the captain's orders," Hughes replied. "Certainly not at a time like this." He led the diplomat's son to the wheelhouse.

The captain and several officers stood on the bridge, peering intently forward through binoculars. Below them, the foredeck was dotted with lookouts as well.

"Captain, I've brought the ambassador's son."

"Thank you," said Rostron briskly. "We need every pair of eyes we can get."

Drazen was still in the dark. "But what are we looking for?"

The captain pointed off the starboard bow. "That."

A mountain appeared out of the darkness, illuminated by the ship's running lights. It towered two hundred feet out of the water, and radiated a blast of cold that was palpable even on this frigid night.

Drazen was no seaman, and it took him a moment to recognize the immense shadow for what it was. "Ice."

Rostron nodded. "And we'll only see more of it the farther north we get. Will you help us?"

The *Carpathia* had always seemed enormous to Drazen. Yet now he had a horrifying image of what would happen if the ship collided with a monster like the iceberg they were passing. The steamer would be nothing more than a thin scattering of broken Christmas tree ornaments floating on the vast ocean.

"Yes, of course," he promised. At that very instant, he caught a faint green flicker on the iceberg's bulk. "Captain, I must be mistaken, but —"

"I saw it, too," interrupted First Officer Dean. "A green light, very low on the horizon."

"A flare!" Rostron exclaimed intently. "Concentrate, gentlemen. We may not be too late after all!"

☆

The flare caused a great stir of excitement on the overturned Collapsible B. Hope lent verve to thirty debilitated and bone-weary survivors. Stiff bodies twisted in the direction of the green light. The motion set the upturned hull rocking, and icy waves washed over them. Panic added to the squirming, setting the unstable craft even further out of balance.

"Be still!" bellowed Lightoller.

"But the flare!" Paddy exclaimed, his feeble voice brimming with hope. "Is it a rescue ship?"

The mere mention of the magic word — rescue — had people scrambling for a better view.

"The next man who moves will be tossed overboard!" roared the second officer. "That is not a rescue ship! Nor will you live to see one if you scuttle us!" He waited until the commotion died down, and then continued in a lower tone: "We are all afloat because the upturned Engelhardt has a pocket of air trapped beneath it. Every motion of the boat and the sea around it will shrink that pocket, causing our perch to sink a little further. I don't believe I need to tell you what that means. When the air is gone, so shall we be."

"But there's a steamer nearby!" came a protest from the stern. "We all saw the flare!"

"That flare was very close," Lightoller explained. "It came from one of our own lifeboats."

It was more than a sigh of disappointment. Paddy could almost feel the life force ebbing from this forlorn group. If they lost the will to soldier on, they were surely doomed.

"Mr. Lightoller," Paddy ventured, "is there any hope at all for us?"

"Several steamers answered our C-Q-D," supplied a voice. It was hard to see assistant Marconi operator Harold Bride, who was lying across the hull, buried by several other men. "The *Carpathia* is closest."

"*Carpathia*?" Lightoller pounced on this information. "Tell me about her."

Jack Phillips, Bride's superior in the wireless shack, raised a bedraggled head, his hair full of ice crystals. "She's a wallowing scow with no speed to speak of, sir. She won't be here until daybreak at the soonest."

"Daybreak!" mourned a member of the galley staff. "We'll be at the bottom of the sea long before then!"

"I'm senior aboard this vessel, such as it is!" Lightoller snapped. "Hear me! There will be no dying without my permission! Our one job is to maintain our air pocket, and to do that we have to maintain perfect balance."

As Paddy watched in amazement, Lightoller organized everyone to stand in two ranks along the overturned hull. Only Bride, who was badly crushed and frostbitten, could not make it to his feet, and even he was placed in a strategic position along the central spine. Then, with Lightoller acting as boatswain, they bobbed into the night, according to the seasoned sailor's reading of the sea.

"Lean to the left! . . . Lean to the right! . . . Stand straight! . . ."

Paddy obeyed along with all the others, sandwiched in frozen misery in the column of sodden, shivering bodies. He could not tear his eyes from the second officer. Charles Herbert Lightoller was inflexible, tyrannical, and the sourest man alive.

But tonight he was their last best hope.

CHAPTER FIFTEEN

Alfie and Sophie used their cupped hands to bail water out of the cupboards of the floating pantry.

"I saved a jar for bailing," Alfie apologized, "but I had to break it over Masterson's head."

"I'll have Mother write a letter of protest to the White Star Line," Sophie quipped. "Protesting is her strong suit."

"So your ma made it to one of the boats," Alfie commented. "That's good."

Sophie squinted through the gloom, reading the pain in his expression. "Your dad didn't." It was not a question.

"He didn't even try," Alfie confirmed bitterly. "He was at his post right to the end, for all that it helped."

"Maybe it helped him to think he was doing the right thing," she soothed. "I — I don't know what happened to Paddy, though. He went overboard when I did. And I haven't seen Julie."

"Miss Julie's on a lifeboat," Alfie told her. "I don't think the earl made it, though."

"So many didn't make it." Sophie shook her head. "The sound of those people in the water —"

Both paused, realizing for the first time that the sound was now gone. Had any of those souls been picked up by the lifeboats? Perhaps a few. The rest were silent because they were dead.

"Oh, my God, Alfie," she wailed. "What's happened here?"

They huddled together for warmth and comfort, mourning the hundreds who had died, and wondering if they would soon be joining their numbers. They'd been told that, in this dazzling new twentieth century, distress calls sent out by Marconi wireless would have dozens of ships steaming to their rescue. Yet they'd also been told that the *Titanic* was unsinkable. Could any of it be believed? And even if ships were coming, how long would it take them to find a ragtag group of survivors floating in an ocean thousands of miles wide? By the time they got here, would everybody be dead of exposure and thirst?

"Your teeth are chattering," Alfie told her.

"I'm so very cold!" It was at that moment that Sophie noticed something. Alfie was no longer shivering. His bare hands were not even in the pockets of his uniform coat. "Aren't you frozen?"

"Of course I am," Alfie replied automatically.

"You don't look it."

"Well, I — I —" A surprised look came over his face as he took stock of himself. "Come to think of it, it's not so bad. Maybe it's getting warmer."

"It's not!" Sophie assured him with growing concern. "You're soaked to the skin, and the air is well below freezing!"

"I'm probably getting used to it," he suggested with a yawn.

Sophie's finishing school had taught nursing skills this past term. One lesson had been the effects of extreme cold on the human body. It was called hypothermia, and its symptoms included a feeling of warmth and comfort when no such feeling should exist. Drowsiness was another. Yes, they were tired. But no one could be sleepy soaking wet, ice cold, and in mortal danger.

Alfie was in trouble.

"*Help!*" she shouted into the pitch-black night. "*Is anybody out there? We need help!*"

"I don't think anyone can hear you," Alfie said mildly.

"*Help!*" Sophie had seen her mother preside over a rally thousands strong by the sheer power of her voice.

If that volume is within me, I must summon it now!

Sophie Bronson shouted, screamed, begged, cajoled, and bellowed until the very waves rang with her cries. Alfie just watched, bemused, but made no comment. He was humming now — the same ragtime tune that the orchestra had played during the loading of the lifeboats. Sophie took a short break and began howling again.

"Boat ahoy!" came a distinct call.

She'd done it! Someone was coming! "*Over here!*" she hollered, scanning the darkness. She could not see the boat, but she could hear the oars splashing clumsily in the water — amateur rowers. A few seconds later, the silhouette was there, blocking the stars just above the horizon.

"Sophie," came a voice, "is that you?"

Sophie felt a rush of emotion. "Julie! Alfie's with me! He needs to get warm!" She could see it now, one of the *Titanic*'s lifeboats, sitting low in the water, dangerously full. She spotted Juliana, with the sleeping child on her shoulder.

"We're all cold, miss," said the young crewman in command.

"It's Junior Steward Huggins," Sophie called. "He shows signs of hypothermia. Can you take us aboard?"

"We've no room, miss. But we can take you in tow so you won't drift away."

Sophie was alarmed. "That's not good enough! He'll die!"

"I'm fine," Alfie insisted vaguely and continued his humming.

Juliana handed the baby to the woman beside her, shrugged out of her cloak, and tossed it onto the floating pantry. "Take my wrap. At least it's dry."

Sophie grabbed it gratefully, and arranged it around Alfie's shoulders.

"Look!" said someone in the crowded lifeboat. "A shooting star!"

"Or distant lightning," offered the crewman.

"That's not it!" exclaimed Juliana, tense with discovery. "It's a light! And it's moving!"

All eyes focused on the phantom glimmer.

"If it's really a steamer," said the crewman

skeptically, "then the flickering should stop as her masthead clears the horizon."

Sophie watched, trembling with hope. Alfie tried to concentrate, peering into the night. Juliana, shivering in her thin gown, began to pray softly, and several other voices joined in.

It was only a few minutes, but it felt like an hour before the distant twinkle resolved itself into a steady beam.

Help was on the way.

CHAPTER SIXTEEN

"The next man who turns around without my permission is going in the drink!" exclaimed Second Officer Lightoller.

In the past hour, the overturned collapsible had sunk inch by inch as the precious air pocket lost its volume. The occupants were now standing knee-deep in water, with the roughening seas washing up to their waists. No longer could Harold Bride recline on the deck and still keep his head above water. Lightoller had him hauled to his feet, and wedged between two of the stronger standees.

"But, sir," Paddy protested, "you saw the lights! That's a rescue ship!"

"Perhaps. But staring at her isn't going to make her come any faster. Make no mistake — this ordeal is not over. It might not be over by half. Consider the number of boats in the water, the number of persons who must be taken aboard. We must survive until our turn comes. And we can only do that by preserving our air pocket. Now, lean to the left!"

Standing on frostbitten feet, Paddy felt his surging hope ebb away with the second officer's harsh words. Not half over? Lightoller was a bully, but no one could doubt the man's seamanship. Of course it would take time to unload survivors from twenty lifeboats scattered across miles of ocean. If they were one of the last to be spotted, rescue could still be hours away.

He looked down and could no longer see his submerged boots. The overturned collapsible would not remain afloat for hours. If it took that much time, they'd be swimming. And enough corpses had floated by the Engelhardt for Paddy to understand the meaning of that.

At least then I won't have to listen to Lightoller anymore.

Who was he kidding? If he died here, it was a sure bet that he'd show up at the pearly gates to find the second officer organizing the lineup, threatening to report slackers to Saint Peter.

Maybe it'll be here sooner than we think. The devil take Lightoller! I'm going to look at the rescue ship!

Both masthead lights were visible now, one over

the other. And the motion was clearly discernible. She was coming, and coming fast.

Then something strange happened. The lights began to wink in and out. Paddy blinked, then squinted. His night sight returned slowly, and he realized the cause of the strange effect. The lights were not flashing on and off. Something was passing between the Engelhardt and the rescue ship. He could make out the silhouettes of heads lined up close to the surface of the water.

"I told you not to turn around, boy!" Lightoller rasped.

"Lifeboats!" Paddy exclaimed in wonder. "A whole string of them! Look!"

Lightoller peered into the gloom. "You really *are* lucky!" The second officer cupped his hands to his mouth, and called out, *"Boat ahoy!"* Yet the night of yelling orders had robbed him of his usual strident voice. All thirty began to cry out at the top of their lungs, but even as a group they could not create enough sound to carry across the water. Cursing in frustration, Lightoller fished a silver whistle from his pocket and brought it to his lips.

☆

In Boat 12, the last thing Seaman Frederick Clench expected to hear was the shrill whistle of the officer of the watch. The *Titanic* was long gone, so he almost doubted his own ears, as if he were hearing a phantom call from beyond the grave. But it persisted, and the passengers were hearing it, too. Someone was out there, clearly calling for help.

Was it Fifth Officer Lowe? He was the one who had created the tiny flotilla of four lifeboats, reasoning that a passing steamer would be quicker to spot a larger object than a smaller one. Lowe had gone off on his own to look for struggling swimmers. Had something gone wrong with that mission? Did the rescuer now need rescue?

Clench scoured the darkness in the direction of the sound until his eyes fell upon the strangest sight he had ever seen in all his years at sea. A crowd of men, dozens strong, appeared to be *standing* on the surface of the water.

"Do you see it, too?" exclaimed the woman beside him. "What's holding them up?"

Clench was a practical man. "They have to be perched on something that's sinking." He and another seaman detached Boats 4 and 12 from the group, and began rowing toward the knot of standees.

As he grew closer, the appalling plight of these poor men struck him like a hammer blow. Their gaunt faces were frozen in stark-white death masks, full of terror and suffering. Several of them seemed to be only semiconscious.

Second Officer Lightoller called out, "You're coming too hard! We're on the hull of an upturned boat, and it won't take much to sink us!"

"Aye, sir." The seaman maneuvered alongside with skill and finesse. He received a cheer from the men that was so faint as to be almost inaudible. Clench knew that, had he heard the whistle ten minutes later, there might have been no one left to take aboard.

Exhausted as he was, Lightoller assumed command, taking charge of an incredibly delicate operation. Every time a man was transferred to one of the lifeboats, those who remained had to rebalance themselves as the Engelhardt sank further. Many lacked the strength to swing a leg over the side, and had to be physically lifted.

To everyone's amazement, a bedraggled figure hanging in the water off the stern of the overturned collapsible abandoned his hold and swam the few strokes over to Boat 4. All transfers halted as everyone watched Chief Baker Charles Joughin haul himself over the gunwale and tumble aboard.

"Good God, man!" Lightoller exploded. "How long have you been down there?"

The sodden baker looked at him. "Since the sinking." He had survived more than two and a half hours in the icy water that had snuffed out hundreds of lives in a matter of minutes. It may or may not have made a difference, but the baker reeked of whiskey.

Paddy was next. He stepped into the boat, avoiding the helping hand offered by Lightoller. In spite of all that the second officer had done to save their lives, there was no escaping the suspicion that his true intent was to grab the stowaway and fling him into the sea. It was irrational, but to Paddy it was very real.

The last time he'd sat down had been in the *Titanic*'s brig, a lifetime ago. Now, after standing for so long, leaning to the left, leaning to the right, a seat in this lifeboat seemed as luxurious as the throne of King George himself.

It was at that moment, in relative comfort for the first time in so long, that Paddy noticed the first faint streaks lightening the black sky. "Morning!" he exclaimed. "I didn't expect to live to see it!"

"You were right, Phillips," commented Lightoller, as he handed another man aboard. "That steamer should be here just as dawn breaks."

Marconi operator Jack Phillips did not respond to this rare compliment from the *Titanic*'s second officer. He had died of exposure during the night, propped upright in a crowd of thirty, alone and unmourned.

CHAPTER SEVENTEEN

RMS *CARPATHIA* —
MONDAY, APRIL 15, 1912, 3:50 A.M.

The rockets sizzled off the *Carpathia*'s bridge, soared skyward, and burst into a cascade of brilliant stars, lighting up the sea around them.

Drazen peered over the rail, searching, ever searching. They had passed much ice on their mad run north, and there was more scattered around them. What there was not was the RMS *Titanic*. Drazen wasn't sure what this might mean, but he was aware of a nervous edge creeping into the voices of Captain Rostron and his officers.

"We've not yet reached the coordinates, Captain," said First Officer Dean.

"The *Titanic* displaces sixty-six thousand tons," said Rostron grimly. "We should see her by now — if there's anything to see."

Drazen had been doing his best to be quiet and unnoticed. He didn't want to be ordered off the bridge and miss out on this momentous rescue. Yet Rostron's words were just too alarming to ignore.

"But Captain — you said the green flare we saw must have been fired from the upper deck of a steamer."

"I might have been mistaken, lad. The night was very clear. A flare can also come from a lifeboat."

Drazen bit his lip. The *Titanic* couldn't be gone! There were more than two thousand people on board!

Rostron put the engines on standby, allowing the *Carpathia* to glide the remaining distance to the *Titanic*'s last reported position. The officers looked at one another in wordless communication. They were here. The *Titanic* was not. There could be only one possible explanation for that.

The flare was so unexpected that everyone recoiled in shock. In the green light it cast, Drazen clearly made out a small boat in the water, perhaps a quarter mile directly ahead.

"*Captain —*"

"We all saw it," the captain assured him, already directing the helm to maneuver alongside the small craft. It took some time to get there, as it was necessary to circle around an iceberg. At last, they eased up to the wooden boat.

"Stop your engines!" came a shout from below.

Drazen peered over the rail at rows of people — women and children — along with a single seaman. A *lifeboat,* he thought, shattered. *And that means —*

"*The Titanic has gone down with everyone on board!*" a lady wailed.

The crew set about dropping lines, and Fourth Officer Boxhall fastened them to the *Titanic's* Boat 2. Avoiding the iceberg had positioned the steamer's starboard side to the small craft, away from the entrance gangways. That left one final obstacle for the cold and exhausted survivors — a forty-foot climb up a rope ladder to the safety of the deck.

At 4:10 A.M., Miss Elizabeth Allen reached the top and was helped aboard the *Carpathia.*

The first *Titanic* passenger had been rescued.

☆

As night turned to day, the bone-weary castaways got their first look at the Cunard liner that was their salvation. At 8,600 tons gross displacement, the *Carpathia* was hardly the magnificent floating city they had started out on, but no ship had ever looked better to those desperate frozen people.

As the sun cleared the horizon, the lifeboats that were all that remained of the mighty *Titanic* began to row for the smaller steamer's lone smokestack. It reminded Paddy of bees returning to the hive. He stood near the bow of Boat 4, which seemed to be inching toward the liner with agonizing slowness. It was so overcrowded, and wallowed so low, that every swell leaked a little more water over the gunwale. A minor thing compared with what he had endured the previous night, but so close to rescue, wet feet seemed like an insult from fate.

At long last, Boat 4 rounded the *Carpathia*'s stern. It came alongside and tied up to the steamer's lines. Ten yards ahead, at the base of a long rope ladder, was another boat, secured and waiting. Lashed to its gunwale bobbed a peculiar floating object that resembled a piece of furniture — shelving, perhaps, like a bookcase. The two figures atop it were soaked and bedraggled. But when the nearer of the two turned his head in Paddy's direction, recognition brought instant joy.

"Alfie! Alfie, it's me!"

Alfie smiled feebly, and waved.

The second figure turned sharply. It was Sophie. "Paddy, you're alive!"

Next he spied Juliana aboard the lifeboat. The child Paddy had saved from steerage was still in her arms. "Paddy, thank God! I thought we were all lost!"

Imagine the four of us, making it through a night like that! Paddy reflected, his heart swelling. *Lightoller called me lucky. Right he was about that.*

Yet he couldn't get past the feeling that the girls might be trying to tell him something. Whatever their secret, Alfie didn't seem to be privy to it. Maybe it was a female thing.

Following shouted instructions from the *Carpathia*'s deck, Sophie was the first to climb the rope ladder. It seemed like an insane thing to ask of a young girl who had spent the night fighting for her life in more ways than the *Carpathia*'s captain could possibly envision. Yet up she went, with a level of grit and determination that would have made her suffragist mother proud.

Alfie's turn was next. It was apparent from the start that the young steward was very weak, and was having a lot of trouble just getting to his feet on the bobbing pantry. At last, he hung on to the rungs of the ladder and heaved himself upright that way.

Watching his friend climb, Paddy knew almost from the start that it was not going to go well. It wasn't merely the frailty of Alfie's movements. That was bad enough. But the young steward seemed vaguely absent, almost unaware of his surroundings.

"Alfie, go back!" shouted Sophie from up on deck. *"They're sending a sling for you!"*

Alfie gave no indication that he had even heard. He managed three more rungs, reaching a height of about twenty feet, before it happened. Paddy would never know if the cause was a sudden movement of the ladder, or perhaps an attack of vertigo. It didn't really matter. The end result was the same. Alfie was disconnected from the ladder, and falling.

His head and shoulders slammed into the edge of the wooden pantry, and he slid off into the sea.

Paddy leaped over the gunwale of Boat 4, and hit the water swimming. This time he barely even noticed the cold, so intent was he on reaching his friend. Alfie's life belt kept him from sinking out of sight, but it was no easy task for the smaller Paddy to haul him back onto the pantry.

Alfie regarded his rescuer vaguely. "You're wet."

Paddy nodded, panting. "You're not so dry yourself."

Alfie seemed completely mystified by that statement. The crewman from Boat 13 joined them on the pantry, and fastened Alfie into the sling. Up soared the young steward, up toward the *Carpathia*'s deck, and the end of this nightmare.

Alfie looked down as Paddy fell away from him, growing smaller by the second.

That boy is soaked and shivering, he thought in concern. *He'd best dry off soon.*

He felt a moment's bewilderment as to where he was being taken. He couldn't just go rushing off like this. He had duties, although at the moment he didn't quite remember what they might be. He seemed to be rising. . . .

At last, he recognized it. He was escorting a first-class passenger up the *Titanic*'s grand staircase, admiring the magnificent stained-glass dome.

"How lovely it is," she said, and he realized to his delight that the lady was his mother.

The sight of her face reminded him that he had something urgent to tell her. "Mum, you don't have to worry about Jack the Ripper anymore."

Da was waiting for them on the landing, dressed like a proper swell in a tailcoat and white tie. "That's fine, boy. Everything's fine."

The orchestra was playing a lively ragtime tune. Alfie knew it, but he couldn't quite recall where he'd heard it before. . . .

☆

Purser Brown reached over the rail and swung the sling onboard the *Carpathia*.

Sophie was right at his side. "Alfie —"

Her breath caught in her throat. Alfie's eyes were open and unseeing.

Brown placed two fingers at the boy's throat, feeling for a pulse. After a moment, he looked up at Sophie, and shook his head sadly.

CHAPTER EIGHTEEN

When Drazen and his father had boarded the *Carpathia* in New York, the liner had been their transportation home to Croatia. Drazen barely recognized the ship now. The saloons had been converted into field hospitals as hundreds of *Titanic* survivors were treated for frostbite and exposure. Spare rooms and compartments had been filled with cots, mattresses, and even sofa cushions to provide additional sleeping quarters. Every passageway seemed to be lined with grim and tragic figures with shocked, tear-streaked faces. It was impossible to pass a hatchway without hearing a sobbing hysterical voice:

"But that *cannot* be the last boat! My husband is not yet aboard!"

Considering that seven hundred and six people had

been saved, there were very few joyous reunions.
More than fifteen hundred had been lost in the sinking of the *Titanic*, more than two-thirds of the souls
aboard the largest liner in the world.

The *Carpathia*'s passengers had donated clothing for the unfortunate newcomers, but even this
simple charity had turned out to be more complicated
than it had seemed at first. The ship had been
bound for the balmy Mediterranean, and the trunks
in the baggage hold contained mostly light linens
and silks, and straw hats. Crew members handed
over their blankets to make up the deficit in
warmth.

Drazen had heard that some of the wealthiest
people in the world were among the survivors. But to
him they looked like ragamuffins, dressed in ill-
fitting garments and draped in bedclothes.

Drazen was helping the kitchen staff by deliver-
ing steaming mugs of soup, coffee, tea, and chocolate.
He was a poor waiter, though. In the overcrowded
passageways, he was jostling elbows and tripping over
feet, spilling hot beverages over a wide area. Luckily
for him, the survivors barely noticed yet another discomfort.

Only a beautiful girl named Juliana complained,

not for herself, but for the small child he'd splashed with cocoa.

"I am most desolately sorry," he apologized formally.

For a moment, the sad girl displayed a dimple. "There is no need to be desolate. There has been ample desolation for one voyage."

"May I help you in some way?" Drazen offered.

She shook her head dispiritedly. "Not unless you can find the parents of this poor child. No one even recognizes her. I fear her family is among the lost."

She picked up the little girl and began to ascend the companion stair.

"Miss," he said quickly. "I believe the steerage passengers are being asked to remain on this deck."

Juliana wheeled on him, her face flushed. "I am a *first*-class passenger!"

Drazen was abashed. The girl was wrapped in a voluminous cloth cloak that had seen better days. Her hair was down — if you could call it that. Long blond strands, matted and wild, framed her petite features like a disorganized sunburst. But of course, a bedraggled appearance meant nothing aboard the

Carpathia. And he should have noticed her cultured speech. . . .

"I — I apologize —"

"My father is the seventeenth Earl of Glamford! At least, he *was* —" Her outrage crumpled. "And a great deal of use his title was to him when the *Titanic* sank! The sea had no more mercy for him than it did for my friend Alfie, who was just a steward!"

She ran off, and he let her go, feeling trivial. In his entire fourteen years, he had not encountered the kind of troubles that these people had suffered in the past half day. What comfort could he possibly offer?

"Sophie-e-e-e-e!"

Amelia Bronson charged across the afterdeck to embrace the daughter she'd thought she'd lost forever. From the moment of her rescue, the renowned suffragist had refused all assistance and even hot food and drink in favor of prowling the *Carpathia*'s decks in search of Sophie. These had been the most difficult, agonizing hours she could remember.

Sophie hugged her mother, her emotions wavering between happiness and sheer amazement. Mother had not wept at either of her parents' funerals; she had not shed a tear when her mentor, the legendary Emmeline Pankhurst, had been clapped in irons; she had not even cried when riot police had broken her nose with a truncheon at one of her rallies. Mother *never* cried.

She was crying now, bawling like a heartbroken child. "I thought I'd lost you! When the ship sank, I thought you were on board!"

"I was." Sophie shrank a little into the waterproof tarpaulin she was using as a cloak. "But that's a story for another day. Please calm down. We both made it, and not everybody did. Alfie —" Two big tears trailed down her cheeks. "Alfie saved my life, but he couldn't save his own."

"I'm so sorry," Amelia sympathized. "He was a fine young man. And Paddy and Juliana?"

"Safe," Sophie reported. "The earl didn't make it, though."

"I've seen Mountjoy," her mother reported. "He's making himself useful in the hospital. I swear they could use that man as an anesthetic! He's the most boring person who ever lived! I haven't seen your cripple, though. Masterson. Nasty man! Although no one deserves to die for that reason."

So Mother had believed her no more than had Captain Smith when Sophie had revealed Masterson's secret identity aboard the sinking *Titanic*. Understandable, perhaps, considering the harrowing chaos of the moment. It had taken the greatest maritime disaster in history to exact justice for Jack the Ripper.

Amelia's face darkened. "You'll never believe who else is on board. Ismay, managing director of the White Star Line! He didn't have enough lifeboat space for everybody, but you'll notice he had room for himself! There's already a rumor that the *Titanic* received warnings about ice, yet did not slow down. The officers have all but admitted it! This is exactly the kind of thing that happens when men are in charge of the decisions that affect our lives!"

Sophie sighed. "Mother, there's been a terrible tragedy. Let's not turn it into a political rally."

And for once, Amelia Bronson agreed.

Off the starboard bow, they watched the arrival of the second ship to respond to the *Titanic* disaster. This was the RMS *Californian*, here to take over the search and salvage operations while the *Carpathia* bore her survivors to New York.

The new arrival was met with a cheer from the *Carpathia*'s decks. Only a few aboard knew that, last night, the *Californian* had sat idle in the water a scant ten miles away while so many of the passengers and crew of the *Titanic* had met their terrible fate.

The ship that might have saved everyone was here at last to aid in picking up the dead.

CHAPTER NINETEEN

BELFAST —
TUESDAY, APRIL 16, 1912, 6:10 P.M.

The city of Belfast had a lord mayor, a council of aldermen, and many prominent citizens. But there was no question that the most powerful man in town was James Gilhooley. The notorious gangster's criminal empire controlled the shipyards, which were the life's blood of the entire city and the two counties beyond.

As he walked down bustling Victoria Street, with its electric trolleys and horse-drawn carriages, Gilhooley was trailed by two bodyguards. Passersby tipped their hats out of respect. Even the newsboy who sold him his evening paper did not expect payment.

The gangster was normally friendly and generous with his gratuity. But today's headline very nearly stopped his heart.

TITANIC FOUNDERS
1500 LOST

Kevin was on the *Titanic*! His beloved brother! How would he ever explain to their elderly mother that he had allowed something to happen to her baby?

His men half-carried him to Donovan's Bar and Grill, the defunct tavern that served as his head-quarters. There at the bar, he read through the lead story of the *Belfast Telegraph* three times.

It told him very little more than the headline had. Four days out of Queenstown, the pride of the White Star Line had struck an iceberg and sunk by the head, with massive loss of life. There were names mentioned — filthy rich Americans, and English and European aristocrats. Astor, Straus, Guggenheim, the Earl of Glamford. All dead. There were seven hundred survivors, but these were mostly women and children.

The barman read over his shoulder. "It says nearly a third of them were saved and taken aboard this other ship. Keep a good thought, boss. Kevin, and Seamus, too — they can look after themselves."

"They were locked in a cell when last I heard from them," Gilhooley moaned. "What chance did a pair of Irish prisoners have when names like Astor didn't get out alive?" He snorted. "Unsinkable, they said! I've half a mind to go over to Harland and Wolff and burn their cursed shipyard to the ground!"

"Unsinkable?" came a small voice. A pale, gaunt boy of fifteen years poked his head out of the storeroom where he'd been sweeping. His name was Daniel Sullivan.

Daniel, the friend Paddy had left behind, and mourned as dead.

While Paddy believed that the Gilhooleys had murdered Daniel, the reality was, in a way, even crueler. The gang had kept the boy as an unpaid drudge — almost a slave.

"You said 'unsinkable,'" Daniel repeated. "Sir, is there news about the *Titanic*?"

The barman motioned him away. "Get back to work, wharf rat!"

"Enough!" exclaimed James Gilhooley wearily. "There's cruelty aplenty in the reality of what's happened." He held up the paper. "Can you read, boy?"

Daniel took in the headline. "Paddy —" It was barely a whisper.

"Aye. Your friend's most surely dead. A stowaway

would have even less chance than my brother to get on a lifeboat. His status on that ship would have been lower than a sack of potatoes in the galley."

It took all of Daniel's willpower to keep from throwing himself full-length onto the barroom floor, and kicking and screaming with grief and outrage. His existence under Gilhooley's iron fist was utterly miserable and without hope for the future. The one bright spot was the knowledge that Paddy was sailing off toward a better life in America. Now that dream lay dead at the bottom of the Atlantic Ocean.

Daniel looked at the two faces in front of him — angry, brutal men who found amusement in tormenting him. The thought of Paddy's good fortune had been everything to him — the reason he opened his eyes every morning. What was left for Daniel Sullivan now?

Poor Paddy. Poor Paddy.

☆

Paddy Burns had known two best friends in this life. First there had been Daniel, who had been killed by the Gilhooleys because of Paddy's recklessness. More recently, there was Alfie, who had died just a few feet short of the safety of the *Carpathia*'s deck.

"I could have saved him," Paddy said grimly. "I could have swum over there and helped him up the ladder. He didn't have to fall."

"Paddy, that's nonsense!" Juliana exclaimed, spooning a soft-boiled egg into the mouth of the little girl who was now always with her. "Alfie didn't die because he fell; he fell because he was dying!"

The girls had been telling him things like this ever since the *Carpathia* had navigated the ice field on her way back to New York. In another day and a half, Captain Rostron said, this whole ordeal would be over. The survivors would sail into New York harbor and begin to put their lives back together as best they might.

"Come to Boston with us, Paddy," Sophie coaxed. "You don't know anyone in New York."

Paddy shook his head. "The last thing you want to be is my friend. All my friends die, they do. Mrs. Rankin is in the hospital under sedation. Aidan and Curran didn't get onto a lifeboat."

"*We're* your friends," Sophie said, almost angrily. "And in case you haven't noticed, we're not dead. Isn't that right, Julie?"

Juliana stroked the little girl's dark hair. "Do you

think I should have the ship's surgeon examine her? She's not said so much as a word."

☆

Paddy had not attended the memorial service held by Captain Rostron the previous day. The entire *Carpathia* was a floating memorial chapel, anyway, and he had seen enough of grieving widows and weeping children. That wasn't likely to stop because some fancy Englishman with epaulets on his shoulders stood up and said nice things about dead people he had never known.

He shook himself a little. *My God, Paddy, you're turning into a cranky old man at fourteen!* Yet he could not come up with an earthly reason *not* to be cranky. And Juliana fretted over why the child wasn't talking! At two years old, that little girl had already seen more horror than would most people over a lifetime.

In many ways, last night's disaster had actually *improved* Paddy's prospects. He'd been in the *Titanic*'s brig, arrested as a stowaway. Now he was just another survivor of the greatest shipwreck in history. He would still arrive in New York with no ticket and no passport — but now he would be accompanied by more than seven hundred people in the identical position. Even his donated makeshift attire was no different from the stolen clothing it had replaced, and his shoes were a change for the better after those ancient hobnail boots. If anything, the sinking represented a step up for him.

A step up that had come at a cost of fifteen hundred lives.

He would have freely and gladly walked into another cell if it could have brought Alfie back.

After the *Titanic*, he found the teeming *Carpathia* maddeningly small. In search of room to breathe, he wandered topside and encountered yet another crowd. A line snaked along the rail, winding across the deck and leading into the wireless shack. The captain had ordered that no more Marconigrams would be transmitted to the hundreds of news services that were clamoring for details. Instead, survivors would be allowed to send wireless messages to loved ones without charge. The response had been overwhelming, and operator Bride of the *Titanic* had been carried from the hospital to the Marconi Room to help Cottam with the workload.

A nice man, was Captain Rostron — not that Paddy had seen much of him. As a *Titanic* stowaway, he was not quite sure what his status was here. He did not wish to tempt fate by bringing himself to the attention of the master of the *Carpathia*. But his eavesdropping told him that Rostron was considered a great hero. Had it not been for the *Carpathia*'s midnight dash through dangerous iceberg-strewn waters, the loss of life might have been near total.

Paddy was about to sidle past, face averted, when a tall figure standing head and shoulders above everyone else caught his eye. He risked a closer look. Broken nose, pockmarked face . . . Seamus! And Kevin Gilhooley standing beside him!

Of all the decent innocent people who had suffered and died in this disaster, fate had spared two murderous gangsters!

At that moment, Gilhooley glanced up, and Paddy knew that Daniel's murderer had spotted him. Gilhooley said something to Seamus. Paddy saw the big bodyguard start toward him, and waited to see no more.

He dashed down a companion stair, and emerged two decks lower, racing along a passageway of first-class staterooms. At least, he thought it must be first class. It was nowhere near as opulent as what the *Titanic* had offered her rich swells — with the obvious advantage that this accommodation was still afloat.

He rounded a corner and collided with an enormous mountain of donated clothing. A group of maids were sorting through the pile, hanging dresses, shirts, and trousers on a large wheeled rack.

"Watch what you're about, boy!" cried one woman sharply. "We're short of clean clothes as it is!"

Paddy reversed course and sprinted back down the corridor, praying he'd be out and gone before Seamus made it this far. He heard very heavy footfalls and saw the henchman's enormous boots clomping down the steps. There was only one hatchway, and he took it, pounding through the main saloon. Folding cots were lined up in rows, each one occupied by a survivor covered up to the neck. Kitchen staff ran in and out, bearing armloads of blankets that had been heated in the galley ovens.

The *Carpathia*'s surgeon, Dr. McGee, stepped in front of him. "Can I help you, young fellow?"

"I came to see Mrs. Rankin."

The doctor nodded. "Very sad case," he said, and pointed to a corner cot.

Paddy started in that direction, but then doubled back and slipped into a screened-off area on the far side of the saloon. Nine cots were set up there, six occupied. But these patients were completely covered.

This is where they bring the dead, he thought. Like Alfie and Jack Phillips, there were several who had survived the sinking only to succumb to exposure aboard the rescue ship.

Paddy had no fear of this place, for no dead man had ever hurt him. It was the living that you had to watch out for.

He froze as Seamus's low rumble reached him from the other side of the screen.

"Did a boy just come running in here?"

Paddy pulled aside the sheet on one of the empty cots, and prepared to leap in and join the ranks of the casualties.

He heard Dr. McGee reply, "Yes, there was one. But I don't see him anymore, so he must have gone."

Paddy stood in mute amazement. They were still chasing him, even after everything that had happened. Why, oh why had he let them out of the brig back on the sinking *Titanic*? He should have remembered the word from the streets of Belfast — if you crossed the Gilhooleys, you were paid back, no matter how long it took. Now these gangsters were chasing him all the way to the New World.

It seemed to Paddy that he had been running and hiding forever — from his stepfather, from the

Belfast police, from Gilhooley and the *Titanic* crew. Now here he was, aboard a new ship, thousands of miles from Ireland, with the *Titanic* sunk and gone, and the deadly game of hide-and-seek was still going on.

CHAPTER TWENTY

NEW YORK CITY, PIER 54 —
THURSDAY, APRIL 18, 1912, 8:00 P.M.

The arrival of the *Carpathia* was the most widely anticipated event of the new twentieth century. More than 40,000 people braved a cold soaking downpour to welcome the Cunarder, her heroic captain, and the *Titanic* survivors.

The newspapers and press services were especially rabid. For the past three days, they'd known of the disaster, but not the details. Most of them had published at least one headline that was entirely made up and utterly wrong: ALL SAVED FROM *TITANIC* AFTER COLLISION; *CARPATHIA* TOWS DIS-ABLED *TITANIC* TO HALIFAX; *CARPATHIA* TRAPPED IN ICE WITH *TITANIC* SURVIVORS.

Now not only were the rescued passengers and crew coming to port but they were bringing with them the true story.

The first view of the distant ship ignited a murmur of excitement and speculation. There was the single smokestack, surrounded by an armada of smaller craft. Photographers' magnesium flares lit up the night, but the steamer's progress seemed agonizingly slow.

The buzz of anticipation turned to cries of dismay when the ship sailed right past the Cunard pier. What was going on here? Why wasn't the *Carpathia* stopping? Was Rostron taking the survivors to a private landing, away from the public view?

The crowd watched in amazement as the steamer approached the White Star dock. There she stopped, lowered the *Titanic*'s lifeboats into the water, and left them bobbing there. Then she returned to the Cunard berth and eased expertly into place.

There was a stampede for the pier building. The entrance was blocked by a line of New York City police officers. Inside, families waited for the *Titanic*'s passengers to set foot on American soil. Tension was unbearably high. Survivor lists had been published, but these were by no means complete or even correct. Many of the relatives inside Pier 54 had no idea if their loved ones were dead or alive. For them, the next hour would be one of spectacular joy or unbearable grief.

They could only wait and pray.

☆

As the *Carpathia*'s gangway was lowered, the mood among the survivors was a mixture of relief and panic. Captain Rostron had ordered that no one who was not being met would be allowed to leave the ship. Many of the *Titanic*'s steerage passengers were immigrants who had no contacts in the new world. They were terrified that they might be taken to Ellis Island, with its notorious holding pens and harsh treatment. Every passport, every identifying paper, and all their earthly possessions lay at the bottom of the ocean with the *Titanic*. To be sent back to Europe after the horrors they'd been through would have been more than they could bear.

"Hurry up, Sophie," urged Amelia Bronson. "Your father will be waiting on the pier. I'm sure he's been here since he received our Marconigram."

It had already been decided that Juliana would disembark with the Bronsons. No one had spoken of the child in her care, but it was understood that Juliana did not intend to part with her. The little girl's family was clearly no longer alive — probably among the hundreds of steerage passengers who had become lost trying to make their way to the *Titanic*'s boat deck during those critical hours. It was impossible to know whether they had been trapped in the maze of passageways, or if they had reached topside only to find the boats all gone. Juliana could only hope that, somewhere, in a life beyond this one, those poor parents were aware that their baby daughter was alive and well, and with someone who loved her.

"I'm not leaving without Paddy," Sophie announced with a determination in her voice that her mother found startlingly familiar. "I refuse to abandon him to wander around here until someone remembers he was a stowaway."

"But the stewards have assembled all the *Titanic* survivors," Juliana protested. "Where could he be?"

"For pity's sake, Julie. This is Paddy we're talking about. He hid aboard the *Titanic* since before it sailed, and no one was the wiser. He could be *anywhere*."

As the remnants of the *Titanic*'s passengers and crew disembarked to tearful reunions, banks of flowers, and hundreds of camera flashes, the Bronsons and Juliana scoured the *Carpathia* for their young Irish companion. But Paddy was nowhere to be found.

It was with heavy hearts that at last they started down the gangway, admitting defeat.

"Miss Juliana!" came an urgent voice from behind them. "Wait!"

Drazen Curcovic ran up to them and handed Juliana

a twice folded paper. It was a Marconi slip, bearing a short and simple message, printed with great care.

GODSPEED — P

"From Paddy?" Sophie prompted. When the diplomat's son looked blank, she added, "Our friend! The Irish boy!"

"Where is he?" added Juliana.

Drazen shrugged. "He gave this to me before we docked. I have been looking for you ever since."

"But did he get off the ship?" Sophie asked in frustration.

"This I cannot tell you," Drazen admitted. "But I have not seen him."

Amelia took the note from her daughter and examined it. "This is all we're going to get from Paddy, I'm afraid."

"But 'Godspeed'?" Sophie echoed. "That doesn't tell us anything!"

"It tells us that it's all he wants to tell us," her mother insisted. "As much as we may wish to help everyone, there are people who simply prefer not to be helped. He's saying good-bye on his own terms, which is how he does everything. It's quite eloquent, actually."

"But did he get off the ship?" Juliana queried.

"I have no earthly idea," Amelia replied readily. "But whatever path he is following, it is uniquely his. You should expect no less of him."

"Madam," First Officer Dean spoke up. "Your husband is waiting for you, is he not?"

Mrs. Bronson bristled. "Why would you assume that I cannot possibly find my way home without a man simply because I am female?"

Dean sighed. "I'm merely asking you to take pity on him lest he begin to fear that your Marconigram was sent in error."

"That's very thoughtful of you," said Sophie quickly, before her mother could extend the argument.

The reunion with Maxwell Bronson was emotional and loving. For forty-eight awful hours — until the wireless message arrived — Sophie's father had believed his wife and daughter were lost forever. Now he had them in his arms. Similar scenes were being played out all over Pier 54.

Hugging her little charge, Juliana hung back and felt fatherless all over again. Papa had been far from the best of parents, but he had loved her in his way, and she sorely missed him.

A tall, tanned man in an immaculate suit stepped forward and tipped his hat to Juliana. "Lady Juliana?

I recognize you from the photograph your father sent. Jed Hardcastle."

"How do you do?" Juliana murmured coolly. So this was the famous Mr. Hardcastle — the Texas oilman who had bartered one of his sons, it didn't matter which one — for a chance to bask in the reflected glory of an earldom.

Juliana had made up her mind, long before the *Titanic* came to disaster, that she would have nothing to do with this arranged marriage. And now that Papa was lost, there would be no one pressuring her to change her mind.

"Who is the child?" Hardcastle asked, frowning.

"My sister," Juliana replied blandly. No sooner had the words passed her lips than she knew that she would make it so. This rescued orphan would be her adopted little sister.

"I didn't know there was a younger sibling," the Texan said skeptically.

"Nor did I, until this moment," Juliana admitted. "I regret to inform you, sir, that my father, the earl, did not survive the sinking."

Mr. Hardcastle nodded. "My condolences. We had feared this to be so. Tell me, is it true that the heir to the title is a distant cousin?"

"Yes, I believe —" It dawned on her suddenly. Her father's death had removed the title from her immediate family. And Mr. Hardcastle now felt that a marriage to her would not be advantageous to any of his sons. This upstart in high-heeled snakeskin boots and a ridiculous gigantic hat was *rejecting* her!

"Thank you for your kind sympathy." She was smiling sweetly, but her voice was cold steel. "I wish you luck finding another titled bride for one of your sons. I remind you, however, that when the *Titanic* foundered, fate did not differentiate on the basis of title or power or wealth. There are people at the bottom of the sea for whom an oil well would be considered mere pocket change. And now I am taking my little sister home to England."

The Bronsons gathered around her, all three glaring Hardcastle away.

"You'll come to Boston with us, of course," Amelia decided. "You'll need to make a recovery before you attempt another journey."

"That's very kind of you," Juliana replied. "Ruth and I are happy to accept."

She smiled. Ruth Alice Glamm — Ruth for Rodney, Papa's name. Alice after Alfie.

"Rooph," repeated the little girl, her first word ever.

☆

Not far away, in the White Star slip at Pier 54, the lifeboats of the ill-fated *Titanic* bobbed in the water, ignored. No one noticed a slight, shadowy figure emerge from Boat 2, shinny up the weathered pylon, and scamper across the wharf, disappearing into the rainy night.

Paddy Burns had arrived in America.

CHAPTER TWENTY-ONE

New York was a city of fat purses aplenty — large pockets waiting to be picked.

Paddy picked none of them. There was simply too much work to be done.

Every factory, every shop, every delicatessen seemed to be hiring somebody to do something. Deliver packages, bag groceries, sweep up cut hair. Every window had a sign: *HELP WANTED ... JOBS AVAILABLE ... BOY NEEDED ... APPLY WITHIN ...*

After the hunger and hopelessness of Belfast, where he and Daniel had been forced to steal to survive, this place was paradise.

Of course, his life here did not compare to the extravagant luxuries he had witnessed aboard the *Titanic*. He shared a dilapidated flat over a tavern on East 7th Street with several other Irish boys and an indeterminate number of rats. But he had a full belly by day and his own bed by night. He even had a key — imagine that! Patrick Burns in a real home with a real door and a lock on it!

Besides, the *Titanic* was surely none too appealing after two weeks on the bottom of the ocean. Her luxuries belonged to the fish now — and the dead. According to the newspapers, a Canadian salvage ship, the *Mackay-Bennett*, had recovered 330 corpses from the wreck site. The remainder, nearly twelve hundred bodies, would forever remain with the one-time pride of the White Star Line in her watery grave.

Paddy was no bookworm, but he pored over every word of those news accounts. He knew, for example, that at the Senate inquiry into the disaster, Second Officer Lightoller had denied abandoning the *Titanic*. His exact words: "I did not leave the ship; the ship left me."

Paddy recalled the very moment Lightoller had been talking about — when the bow had dipped, creating the wave that had washed them all off the boat deck. He pitied the poor American senator who expected to get the best of Charles Herbert Lightoller.

In the end, most of the blame was going to Captain

Smith for ignoring the ice warnings and to the White Star Line for providing too few lifeboats. Bruce Ismay argued that no liner of any company carried sufficient boats to accommodate the full complement of passengers and crew. That was going to change. A new law had already been proposed: All ships must have lifeboat space for everybody, pure and simple.

A fat lot of good that'll do the 1,517 who died that night, Paddy reflected darkly.

He had also read in the society pages that Lady Juliana Glamm, daughter of the late Earl of Glamford, had taken ship for England with the orphaned child she had rescued from the *Titanic*. She'd advanced her departure because her Boston hostess, famed suffragist Amelia Bronson, was in jail again. After Amelia's arrest at a rally in Portland, Maine, her daughter, Sophie, had run out onstage and whipped up the crowd with such skill and passion that she was being called "the next face of the American suffragist."

Godspeed, Paddy had wished them. And speeding they were — off in their own directions. He had a loving thought for Alfie, who was missing all this. The boy who saved America from Jack the Ripper, Sophie had called the young steward. The world would never know what a true hero it had lost.

Mostly, though, Paddy had no time to think about the past. He was just too busy, spreading sawdust on the floor of the butcher shop in the mornings, mucking out stables in the afternoons, and hawking the evening papers on the street. In Belfast, no one had been able to find a job. In New York, he was constantly running between three or four. And the only full pocket on his mind was his own.

At long last, Paddy Burns dared to be happy — until the Gilhooleys began stalking him.

He spotted Seamus first, towering above the crowd in Washington Square Park. There was no mistaking that broken nose, pointing at all four corners of the square at the same time.

An unhappy coincidence it was — everybody went to the park of a Sunday afternoon. Or so thought Paddy.

But the next day, he arrived at the stable to find Seamus and Kevin Gilhooley himself making inquiries of the stablemaster. There went one job. Luckily, here in New York, paid work was plentiful.

Two days later, he was clearing tables at Katz's Delicatessen when they walked in. This time there was nowhere to hide. He was standing in the middle of the dining room in his white apron, weighed down by an enormous tray of dirty dishes and glassware.

Gilhooley hailed him. "We need to talk to you, boy."

"Don't count on it," Paddy snarled, and the tray and its contents were airborne in the gangsters' direction. It was his resignation from Katz's. He was out the back door, never to return. Another lost job, courtesy of the Gilhooleys.

The comfort of his New York life was slipping away. It was Belfast all over again — the constant fleeing from something or somebody.

For the next five days, he tried to lie low, staying in the flat over the tavern, not going to any of his jobs. New York was a city of millions. Surely the Gilhooleys wouldn't make a career out of chasing one boy who had stolen from them literally an ocean away.

Eventually, though, the money ran out, and with it the food. And although Paddy was accustomed to going hungry, there were limits even to that.

His employers welcomed him back without question. Such was the need for workers in this New World.

He was returning home from his newspaper job when he noticed the spanking new Ford Model T parked in front of the tavern. It set off alarm bells. Automobiles were common in New York, but this was more of a horse-drawn or handcart neighborhood.

Too late he spied the hulking form behind the steering wheel. Seamus, with Kevin Gilhooley in the seat beside him.

Paddy ran down 7th Street, expecting to hear heavy footfalls in hot pursuit. Instead, he was shocked by the roar of the engine approaching from the rear and gaining on him. He knew he could defeat those thugs in any footrace, but the automobile changed everything. Within seconds, he could feel the vibration of the motor right behind him.

They're going to run me down!

Blind panic took over, and he ducked into a lane. In an instant, he knew that the decision had undone him. There was no exit to this alley, no doors off it. He was well and truly trapped.

The Model T nosed its way in after him, blocking any hope of escape. There was only one way out — up and over. Paddy took a run at the flivver, leaped onto the hood, and almost made it to the roof. Seamus's long arm snaked out, snagged his ankle, and hurled him back to the pavement. Both gangsters jumped from the car and advanced on him.

"You're a slippery little sewer rat, you are." Kevin Gilhooley laughed. "Can't you let anybody do you a favor?"

"What favor? Murdering me the way you murdered

Daniel?" Paddy picked up a broken brick with a jagged edge. "I may die this day, but I'll take one of you with me, you can count on that!"

"Paddy, *don't!*"

A slender figure jumped from the automobile and rushed out behind Seamus.

Paddy stared. The brick dropped from nerveless fingers. He gaped. He goggled. The image grew fuzzy in front of his eyes.

Daniel Sullivan, in the flesh.

"But you're . . . dead."

Daniel beamed. "I see that a swim in the cold Atlantic hasn't made you any smarter." His tone was joking, but there was a tremor in his voice.

"That's why we've been looking for you, you gaumless idiot," Gilhooley explained with a benevolent smile. "It's your reward. You may remember you saved our lives aboard that cursed English ship."

"To unlock our cell after we tried to do you in," Seamus added. "For a little runt, you've the heart of a lion."

Paddy walked shakily toward his beloved comrade and reached out to touch him on the arm. To his amazement, Daniel did not disappear in a puff of smoke. Amid the chaos and horror of the *Titanic* tragedy,

Paddy had forgotten how alone he'd felt since that terrible day when he'd believed Daniel murdered.

He'd known kindness since then. And friendship. But Daniel was *family*.

Some things defied a price tag and an entry in a cargo manifest — even aboard the greatest ship the world had ever known.

In the past days, Paddy had watched so many die around him. Here at last was one back from the grave. It was a gift.

He blinked rapidly. *Better to be hanged than to cry!* "I really thought you were dead," he murmured. "I saw —"

"You were dead, too," Daniel told him soberly. "When the *Titanic* sank, what was I supposed to think?"

"Like a couple of cats," Kevin Gilhooley observed. "With sixteen lives still left between you. And money, too." He produced a fat purse and handed it to Paddy. "From my brother, with his gratitude."

Daniel aimed a playful punch at Paddy's arm. "This must be the first time anybody ever gave us one of those willingly."

"And we have two jobs for you, if you want them," added Gilhooley.

Paddy shook his head. "This money is for *school*," he declared firmly. "Daniel is going to be an engineer one day. He knew what could sink the *Titanic* before it happened."

"What about you, Paddy?" Daniel prompted. "What are your plans?"

Paddy cast him his customary cheeky grin. "Oh, you don't have to fret about me. I'll get by."

Paddy Burns was a survivor.

GORDON KORMAN started writing novels when he was about the same age as the characters in this book, with his first novel, *This Can't Be Happening at Macdonald Hall!*, published when he was fourteen. Since then, his novels have sold millions of copies around the world. Most recently, he is the author of *Swindle*, *Zoobreak*, and *Framed*, the trilogies Island, Everest, Dive, and Kidnapped, and the series On the Run. His other novels include *No More Dead Dogs* and *Son of the Mob*. He lives in New York with his family, and can be found on the web at **www.gordonkorman.com**.

GO ON MORE THRILLING ADVENTURES WITH
GORDON KORMAN!

In this suspenseful series, teens fight for survival after being shipwrecked on a desert island.

Who will be the youngest person to climb Everest? Find out in this adventure-filled series!

In this action-packed trilogy, four young divers try to salvage sunken treasure without becoming shark bait!

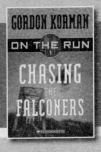

Two kids become fugitives in order to clear their convicted parents' names in this heart-stopping series.

The hunt is on after Aiden's sister is abducted right before his eyes in this action-packed adventure trilogy.

MISFITS
UNITE!

More madcap antics from
GORDON KORMAN